Dummie the Mummy

AND THE TOMB OF AKHNETUT

For Egypt, an extraordinary country

www.dummiethemummy.com

ISBN 978 90 00 35785 7
NUR 284

Originally published in Dutch in 2015 © Van Goor
English translation © 2018 Van Goor
Unieboek | Het Spectrum bv
P.O Box 97
3990 DB Houten, The Netherlands

www.toscamenten.nl
www.beeldvanhees.nl
www.de-leukste-kinderboeken.nl

Text Tosca Menten
Design and illustrations Elly Hees
Translation Michele Hutchinson
Typeset Mat-Zet bv, Soest

Tosca Menten

Dummie the Mummy

AND THE TOMB OF AKHNETUT

With illustrations by Elly Hees

Translated by Michele Hutchinson

Van Goor

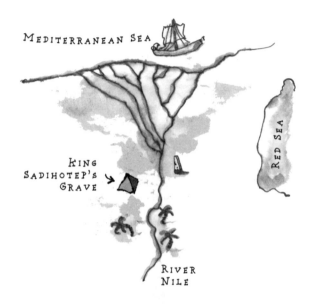

DARWISHI UR-ATUM MSAMAKI MINKABH ISHAQ EBONI
RODE UP THE HILL ON HIS DONKEY AKILA. WHEN HE
REACHED THE TOP, HE GAZED OUT ACROSS THE DESERT.
KING SADIHOTEP THE GREAT, HIS FATHER'S FATHER,
WAS DEAD. THERE IN THE DISTANCE, HIS
GRANDFATHER'S PYRAMID WAS READY AND WAITING. IT
HAD ONLY JUST BEEN COMPLETED. LAST TIME THE NILE
FLOODED, THE BUILDERS HAD TAKEN THE FINAL STONES
TO THE TOP.

DARWISHI HAD EXPECTED HIS GRANDFATHER TO LIVE
FOR MANY MORE YEARS. BUT INSTEAD, ALL OF A
SUDDEN HE'D DIED IN THE MIDDLE OF THE NIGHT.

DARWISHI TURNED AROUND SADLY AND LOOKED AT
THE MIGHTY BLUE-GREEN RIVER NILE. THE FLOODS HAD
ENDED OVER TWO MONTHS AGO AND THE LAND WAS
LUSH AND FERTILE. THEY HAD SADIHOTEP TO THANK FOR
THAT. SADIHOTEP HAD BEEN A GOOD KING. AND A VERY
KIND GRANDFATHER...

EGYPT BELONGED TO DARWISHI'S FATHER AKHNETUT
NOW. HIS FATHER WOULD HAVE TO TAKE CARE OF IT AS
WELL AS SADIHOTEP HAD. AND LATER, WHEN AKHNETUT
WAS GONE, DARWISHI HIMSELF WOULD BE KING AND
THIS FERTILE COUNTRY WOULD BE HIS...

FOR A MOMENT, DARWISHI FELT VERY PROUD. BUT

THEN HE PICTURED HIS GRANDFATHER'S SEVERE BUT
KIND FACE AGAIN. AND IMMEDIATELY AFTER THAT HE
THOUGHT OF THE TERRIBLE ROOM IN WHICH THEY HAD
TURNED HIS GRANDAD INTO A MUMMY. HE SHIVERED. IT
HAD TAKEN SEVENTY DAYS. HIGH PRIEST HEPSETSUT
HAD TAKEN HIM THERE A FEW TIMES. EACH TIME,
HEPSETSUT HAD EXPLAINED WHAT WAS HAPPENING. IT
HAD BEEN A TERRIBLE SHOCK FOR DARWISHI EACH TIME.
THE FIRST TIME, THERE WERE FOUR LARGE JARS NEXT
TO HIS GRANDFATHER'S BODY.

"WHAT PRETTY VASES. WILL THEY BE BURIED WITH
HIM TOO?" DARWISHI HAD ASKED CURIOUSLY.

"THEY ARE FOR HIS BRAINS AND ENTRAILS,"
HEPSETSUT HAD SAID.

"WHAT?!"

DARWISHI HAD RUN AWAY SCREAMING, AND HE HAD
SPENT THE WHOLE DAY THINKING ABOUT THEM TAKING
OUT HIS GRANDAD'S INSIDES AND PUTTING THEM IN THE
VASES.

THE SECOND TIME HE HAD TO GO ALONG, THEY WERE
SPRINKLING WHITE STUFF ALL OVER HIS GRANDAD TO
DRY HIM OUT. AND THE THIRD TIME THEY WERE
SPRAYING ALL KINDS OF OIL ON HIM.

"WHY DO I NEED TO KNOW ALL OF THIS?" DARWISHI
CRIED. "IT'S DREADFUL!"

BECAUSE YOU ARE THE PHARAOH'S OLDEST SON,"
HEPSETSUT SAID. "IT MEANS YOU'LL BE KING YOURSELF
ONE DAY. FROM NOW ON, YOU ARE NOT JUST TO LEARN
THE SECRETS OF LIFE BUT THOSE OF DEATH AS WELL.
WE ARE PREPARING YOUR GRANDFATHER'S BODY FOR HIS
JOURNEY. IF YOUR GRANDFATHER'S BODY IS PRESERVED,

HE CAN TRAVEL ON UNDISTURBED AND LIVE WITH THE GOD OSIRIS FOR ALL ETERNITY."

AND SO HIS GRANDFATHER WAS TRANSFORMED FROM A HANDSOME MAN INTO A WRINKLED MUMMY. AND TODAY HE WOULD BE BURIED.

DARWISHI GUIDED AKILA TO THE TEMPLE BESIDE THE NILE. THERE THE PROGRESSION BEGAN TO MAKE ITS WAY ALONG THE LONG ROAD TO THE PYRAMID.

DARWISHI WAS ALLOWED TO RIDE AKILA IN THE PROCESSION, BECAUSE THE DONKEY HAD BEEN A GIFT FROM HIS GRANDFATHER. IT MEANT HE HAD A GOOD VIEW. HEPSETSUT WAS RIGHT AT THE FRONT. THEN CAME THE OXEN THAT PULLED UP THE BOAT CONTAINING SADIHOTEP, USING ROLLING TREE TRUNKS. BEHIND THEM WALKED THE PRIESTS AND PRIESTESSES BEARING OFFERINGS AND AFTER THEM, HIS FATHER AND MOTHER. AT THE BACK WERE THE PEOPLE WHO LIVED IN THE PALACE WITH THEM, AND THEN CAME THE OTHER PEOPLE. THE PROCESSION WAS NEARLY AS LONG AS THE ENTIRE ROAD.

DARWISHI GLANCED TO THE SIDE. HIS FATHER LOOKED GOOD. AKHNETUT WAS WEARING THE DOUBLE CROWN OF EGYPT, THE WHITE CROWN OF THE SOUTH AND THE RED CROWN OF THE NORTH. IN THE MIDDLE OF THE CROWN, THE POWERFUL GOLDEN SCARAB OF MURATAGARA GLITTERED. AND IN HIS HANDS, AKHNETUT CARRIED A BRAND NEW GOLDEN SCEPTRE. WOULD DARWISHI LOOK LIKE THAT HIMSELF ONE DAY? IT HARDLY SEEMED POSSIBLE.

THEY SLOWLY WALKED ON. IT WAS HALF AN HOUR

BEFORE THE PROCESSION REACHED THE TEMPLE NEXT TO
SADIHOTEP'S PYRAMID. THE SOUND OF PEOPLE WAILING
IN GRIEF GREW LOUDER.

THE BEARERS CAREFULLY LIFTED SADHOTEP'S BODY
FROM THE BOAT AND DISAPPEARED INTO THE PYRAMID
WITH IT.

DARWISHI WAS ALLOWED TO GO WITH THEM INTO THE
LARGE SQUARE BURIAL CHAMBER.

HE SAW EVERYTHING. SADIHOTEP IN HIS STONE
SARCOPHAGUS. THE SCARY JARS. AND ALL THE
TREASURES HIS GRANDAD WAS TAKING WITH HIM,
ALMOST TWO ROOMS FULL. EVEN HIS GRANDAD'S GOLDEN
CHAIR WAS GOING ON HIS JOURNEY WITH HIM.

DARWISHI LOOKED AT THE WALL BEHIND THE
SARCOPHAGUS. HE'D DONE A PICTURE FOR HIS
GRANDFATHER ON IT. HE HAD SPENT TWO WHOLE DAYS
IN THE BURIAL CHAMBER PAINTING THREE ELEGANT
BIRDS WITH LONG NECKS. THEY WERE FLYING ABOVE THE
NILE DURING THE FLOODS. IT WAS THE NICEST PAINTING
IN THE ENTIRE GRAVE, HE THOUGHT PROUDLY.

IT WAS ALMOST OVER. AS THEY CHANTED, THE
PRIESTS MOVED THE HEAVY LID ONTO THE
SARCOPHAGUS. FINALLY, HEPSETSUT PLACED SADIHOTEP'S
GOLDEN SCEPTRE RESPECTFULLY ON HIS SARCOPHAGUS.

THEN THEY WALKED BACKWARDS, BENT OVER,
THROUGH THE PYRAMID'S CORRIDORS UNTIL THEY WERE
OUTSIDE. HEPSETSUT CAME LAST, SMOOTHING OVER THE
SAND WITH HIS FEET AS HE WENT.

OFFERINGS WERE STILL BEING SET DOWN IN
GRANDAD'S TEMPLE. PEOPLE SANG AND DANCED. IT
ALMOST SEEMED LIKE A PARTY, DARWISHI THOUGHT

ANGRILY.

AS THE SUN SET, HEPSETSUT SEALED THE GRAVE AND
THEY FINALLY WENT HOME.

DARWISHI CRIED THE WHOLE NIGHT. HIS GRANDAD HAD
ONLY JUST SET OFF ON HIS JOURNEY, BUT HE MISSED
HIM ALREADY...

EARLY THE NEXT MORNING, HEPSETSUT CAME INTO HIS
BEDROOM.

"COME WITH ME," HE WHISPERED.

DARWISHI GOT UP AND FOLLOWED THE HIGH PRIEST
OUTSIDE. A CARRIER CHAIR WITH SIX BEARERS STOOD
WAITING FOR HIM IN THE DARK.

"WHERE ARE WE GOING?" DARWISHI ASKED.

"OUT."

"OUT? TO THE VILLAGE? WHY?"

HEPSETSUT PUT HIS HAND ON DARWISHI'S HEAD. "ONE
DAY THE CROWN OF EGYPT WILL REST ON YOUR HEAD,"
HE SAID. "YOU WILL BE KING, DARWISHI. THAT'S WHY I
WANT TO SHOW YOU HOW YOUR PEOPLE LIVE, WORK AND
EAT. FROM NOW ON, I'LL TAKE YOU TO THE VILLAGE
EVERY FULL MOON. YOU MUST TAKE GOOD CARE OF THE
PEOPLE WHEN YOU ARE OLDER. YOU WILL LEAD THEIR
ARMY, YOU WILL ADMINISTER THEIR JUSTICE, YOU WILL
ENSURE PEACE, PROSPERITY AND ETERNAL LIFE.
WHETHER THE PEOPLE DO WELL DEPENDS ON YOU. THIS
IS WHY YOU NEED TO GET TO KNOW THEM."

"BUT THEY'RE ORDINARY PEOPLE. WON'T DAD MIND?"
DARWISHI ASKED.

"I DID THE SAME WITH HIM," HEPSETSUT SAID.

THE BEARERS CARRIED LITTLE DARWISHI TO THE

VILLAGE. WHILE THE SUN WAS BORN ON THE OTHER
SIDE OF THE NILE, THEY ENTERED A HOUSE. PEOPLE
WERE EATING BEANS AND DRINKING BEER. WHEN THEY
SAW HEPSETSUT, THEY STOPPED EATING AND BOWED. A
DARK WOMAN WITH BLACK EYES FETCHED A PLATE WITH
THREE FISHES ON IT.

HEPSETSUT GAVE DARWISHI A FISH. IT WAS DRY AND
TASTED OF SALT.

DARWISHI ATE MORE FISH AND AFTER THAT HE HAD
BEANS. A STRANGE WOMAN LAID A FLORAL GARLAND
BEFORE HIM ON THE FLOOR AND A POT OF SCENTED OIL.
DARWISHI NODDED AWKWARDLY AND PICKED IT UP.

AFTER AN HOUR, THEY RETURNED TO THE PALACE.

"FROM NOW ON YOU WILL LEARN TO READ AND
WRITE. I WILL TEACH YOU HOW TO FIGHT IN WARS, HOW
TO SWIM, HOW TO WRESTLE AND HUNT WILD ANIMALS. I
WILL TEACH YOU ABOUT RELIGION," HEPSETSUT SAID.

"BUT I CAN'T DO ANY OF THAT," DARWISHI SAID IN
CONFUSION.

HEPSETSUT SMILED. "I WILL HELP YOU," HE SAID.
"FROM NOW ON, EVERYTHING IS GOING TO BE
DIFFERENT—"

DARWISHI JOLTED AWAKE. HE OPENED HIS EYES, SAT UP
AND LOOKED AROUND. HIS NEW FRIEND ANGUS WAS
ASLEEP NEXT TO HIM. HIS NEW DAD, NICK, WAS LYING
IN THE OTHER BEDROOM. HIS HAND FELT FOR THE

CHAIN WITH THE SCARAB AROUND HIS NECK. IT WAS
THE SCARAB OF MUKATAGARA FROM HIS FATHER'S
CROWN, AND THE ONLY MEMENTO OF HIS FATHER AND
MOTHER HE HAD LEFT.

YET AGAIN HE HAD DREAMED OF THE PAST. AND
AGAIN HE'D ALMOST FORGOTTEN EVERYTHING. IT HAD
BEEN SOMETHING ABOUT A FUNERAL PROCESSION, AND
ABOUT HEPSETSUT. FOR THE PAST FEW DAYS, HE'D
DREAMED EVERY NIGHT. DREAMS ABOUT HIS DONKEY, HIS
FATHER, THE PEOPLE IN EGYPT. BUT WHEN HE WOKE UP,
EVERYTHING WAS GONE. HE WAS NEVER BACK HOME. HE
WOULD NEVER EAT SALTED FISH WITH HEPSETSUT
AGAIN. HE WOULD NEVER BE PHARAOH AND HAVE HIS
OWN PYRAMID. IT WAS FOUR THOUSAND YEARS LATER
AND HE WAS IN A FOREIGN COUNTRY CALLED THE
NETHERLANDS. EVEN HIS NAME WAS DIFFERENT. HE
WASN'T CALLED DARWISHI ANYMORE BUT DUMMIE.

HE SLID OUT OF BED, WENT TO THE MIRROR IN THE
BATHROOM AND LOOKED AT HIS DRIED-OUT FACE WITH
ITS TORN LIPS AND GOLDEN EYES. HE CLOSED HIS EYES.
NOW HE SAW HIS BLACK BRAIDED HAIR, FLAWLESS PALE
BROWN SKIN AND PEARLY WHITE TEETH. WHEN HE
OPENED HIS EYES AGAIN, HE LOOKED STRAIGHT INTO
THE HOLE WHERE HIS NOSE HAD ONCE BEEN.

AFTER A WHILE HE TURNED AROUND AND WENT BACK
INTO THE BEDROOM. HE QUIETLY SLIPPED BACK INTO BED
AND CLUTCHED HIS SCARAB TIGHTLY IN HIS HAND.

DAD, HE THOUGHT. DAD, MUM. HE COULDN'T GET BACK
TO SLEEP.

CHAPTER 1

A painting of Donkeys

It was hot in Polderdam.

Usually not much happened in the village, but right now it was so hot that nothing happened at all.

Nick Gust was painting in his shed with the door open and Angus was sitting on a bench in the shade and looking at Dummie. He wasn't affected by the weather at all. He had climbed the tree in the garden and was swaying dangerously back and forth at the top. "Come on up!" he called down to Angus. "Ghere in tree is wind!"

"And down here, it's safe!" Angus shouted back.

Indoors the telephone rang.

Dummie let go and fell smack bang onto the ground, before running inside.

"Dummie ghere," Angus heard him say. "No, not Nick. Wait, I gho look." He came back out holding the telephone and walked to the shed.

At that moment Nick appeared in the door opening

holding a paintbrush and muttering. "Ugly cottypot!" he scolded. Angus grinned. "Ugly cottypot" meant that his painting wasn't going well.

"There is man in telephone for you," Dummie said.

"I'm not here," Nick said in annoyance.

"But I see you," Dummie said, amazed.

"That man can't see me. Make something up."

"OK— Mister, Nick says ghe may be on toilet. Or somewhere else, I can make it up. No, no joke, ghe says it himself."

Angus burst out laughing.

Nick groaned and snatched the telephone from Dummie's hand. "Nick Gust— Yes, I'm busy— No, not on the toilet— What?" All of a sudden his face changed. "Yes, that's right— Really? When? ... This afternoon already? ... Oh, wow— Yes, of course. Fifteen you say? ... Yes, I know where it is. Right. Well, erm, see you later— Goodbye."

He hung up and stared into space, taken aback. "Whumpy dumpman," he muttered.

"What is it, Dad?" Angus asked.

"An exhibition. They asked me to show my work in the old storage depot. Fifteen paintings. They need them this afternoon. Someone dropped out. They got my name somewhere."

"Then I don't suppose they've seen any of your work," Angus giggled. He peered through the door to the back of the shed. Nick painted paintings that never got sold. His whole shed was full of them.

"That's going to change now," Nick said, suddenly excited. "Give me a hand, we're going to choose a few."

The three of them went into the shed. The racks of paintings were near the back wall. They were all differ- ent: big, small, with funny landscapes and sometimes just colours. But to Angus they were all the same: very ugly. He looked through them, one by one, his nose in the air. "Are you sure they're all finished?" he asked doubtfully. "No one's going to buy this stuff."

"It's art, son. You have to learn how to look properly."

"I've been looking at it all my life," Angus said.

"Then you need to look better," Nick said. "Here, where can you see a lovely sky like this?"

"A green sky? Nowhere."

"Fine, listen, if you want to see a blue sky, just look up," Nick grumbled. He took a couple more paintings covered in big splatters from the rack.

Angus thought about the paintings in the Grobbe Museum which he'd been to the previous month with Mr Scribble. He'd seen paintings there with even crazier colours. And with even more splatters, for that matter. And they were in a museum!

"Alright, I suppose you could be right," he said. "This one then. It's the least ugly. And this one. And— Hey! I actually like this one!" He pulled out a big painting from behind the others. "This one is very different. Is it your new style?"

"Is by me," Dummie said proudly. "I made it. Last week, when you were sick."

"You?" Angus' mouth fell open.

Dummie's painting featured three donkeys and men in dresses with clothes on their heads, behind them sand dunes, a couple of pyramids and a low sun. The

long shadows of parched bushes fell onto the sand.
Angus already knew that Dummie was good at drawing,
but he was even better at painting!

"Shall we take this one too?" Angus asked excitedly.

"No," Dummie said immediately.

"Why not? Then everyone will be able to see it. Maybe
someone will even buy it."

"No, I want to keep," Dummie said. "Ghood donkeys."

Nick burst out laughing. "I think it's a good idea. You
know what? We'll take the donkeys along. And they
we'll say the painting costs ten thousand euros. Then
everyone will have seen them, but they will remain
yours. No one would buy a thing like that. It's simply
too expensive."

"Are you sure?" Dummie hesitated. He squeezed his golden eyes half shut and stuck his tongue out of his dried-up mouth.

"Do I know about art or not?" Nick said.

Angus said nothing.

"OK. Maashi," Dummie said. "Donkeys can gho."

It took a while before they'd chosen fourteen paintings of Nick's that they all found the least ugly. Nick put the others back in the racks and rubbed his chin. "They need to have titles as well," he said. "Erm, this one I'll call *White and red*. Do you agree?"

"What about that one next to it then?" Angus giggled.

"*Red and white*, I think," Dummie sniggered.

"Stop it, you two," Nick said crossly. "I'll do this on my own."

He got a piece of paper and listed the fourteen titles. Afterwards, he put the paintings near the door. "We'd better make a quick price list too," he said.

Soon they were sitting at the computer.

Nick began to type.

Price list for the paintings by Nick Gust.
  Number 1: **Red with white.** €1,000
  Number 2: **Green sky.** €1,000

"And what's your painting called?" Nick asked when he'd finished writing down his paintings.

"Is called *My ghome*," Dummie said. "Painting costs ten thousand."

And so it came about that one hot Saturday afternoon, Nick found himself carefully lifting fifteen paintings into a trailer. He had put big sheets over them for protection. Dummie insisted on going along to look after his donkeys and Angus went along to look after Dummie. They drove slowly into the city.

The old storage depot was a building with three meeting rooms and a restaurant.

Nick parked in front of the door. No sooner had he done so when a short man came out. "Are you Mr Gust?" he asked hastily.

"Nick Gust," Nick said. "And this is my son Angus, and that's my nephew Dummie."

"Stephen Curl," the man said. He stared at Dummie in disbelief. "Has he had an accident?" he whispered.

"Burns," Nick whispered back. "He has to be fully bandaged for a while."

Mr Curl shook his head pityingly. But he obviously didn't have time to carry on being amazed, because he said, "Well, let's hang them up quickly. The restaurant will be opening in an hour."

They carried the canvases inside together. Nick lifted a sheet from one of the paintings.

Mr Curl looked at the big splatters of paint in surprise. "That's a little, well— erm, wild," he said uneasily. "It would better for my restaurant if it represented something."

"It actually represents lots of things," Nick said. "You

can read anything into it you like. Birds. A herd of elephants. A bunch of tulips."

"Oh. A bunch of tulips," Mr Curl repeated.

"Yes. But also landscapes, you see. Here, this one, for instance."

Mr Curl stared at the green sky with a grimace. "Oh," he said again.

"Where do you want them?" Nick asked.

Mr Curl hesitated. Then he shook his head determinedly. "I don't want that one in the restaurant," he said. "It'll spoil people's appetites. No one will feel like eating. And I don't want this one either. Do you have anything else?"

Nick crossly pulled one sheet after the next off the paintings. Mr Curl shook his head at each one of them. "Nope. Nope." Then they got to Dummie's painting. "Aha. Now we're talking," Mr Curl said in relief. "At least this one looks like a landscape with donkeys."

"Yes, is desert with donkeys," Dummie said.

"Lovely. It will make the customers thirsty. This one

can go in the restaurant," Mr Curl said. "Do you have any more of these?"

"No," Nick said. As he tugged away the last sheet, Mr Curl continued to shake his head and in the end only Dummie's painting was allowed hang in the restaurant. Nick's paintings had to go in the meeting rooms.

Nick took them to the meeting rooms with a red face.

Angus and Dummie stayed in the restaurant and watched Mr Curl hang Dummie's painting on the back wall. If you stood at the door, you looked right at it. "That's the best place," Angus whispered to Dummie. "Everyone who comes in will see it straight away."

After a while, Nick reappeared in the restaurant and reluctantly handed the price list to Mr Curl.

"Which one is *White and red*?" Mr Curl asked.

"It's one of a pair," Nick growled. "And the other's called *Red and white*."

Mr Curl shook his head for the thousandth time. "Very clear," he muttered. "Well, I'll call you when you can come and pick them up again. Erm... thank you. See you soon." He shook Nick's hand and walked off.

"Whumpy dumpman! I'll never have another show again!" Nick roared when they were back in the car. "That man knows nothing about art. Brainless baldy Curl with his nonsense about appetite."

"My painting ghoes in restaurant," Dummie said proudly.

"As if donkeys will make people hungry," Nick snorted.

"And thirsty," said Dummie. "Is ghot on donkey."

"Oh, whatever. It's hot everywhere!" Nick put his foot

to the floor and the car accelerated.

"Have you ever sat on a donkey?" Angus asked quickly to distract his father.

"Yes. I ghad own donkey. Donkey called AKILA, name means clever. But ghe do what ghe want. Always walking wrong way. Donkey of my dad called ZUBERI. Also do what ghe want. All donkeys do what they want. AZIBO, OLABISI, KASIYA..."

"Shall we give your car a name too, Dad?" Angus asked.

"Yes. Stephen Curl," Nick growled. He turned onto their driveway and stamped so hard on the brakes that the car hurtled to a stop. He got out and stormed into the shed without saying anything else.

"I feel a bit sorry for him," Angus said.

"I don't. My painting is in restaurant," Dummie said.

That evening Nick made potatoes and broccoli for dinner. Angus set the table. As he and his father ate, Dummie played with his scarab. Luckily Nick had already calmed down. He'd even been able to paint away his ill feeling, he said. There were paint stains on his trousers and his forehead was green.

They'd almost finished when the telephone rang.

"I ghet it," said Dummie. "Ghello?" He listened and then looked at Nick. "Mister Curl from Storage Depot is in telephone again," he said.

Nick got up and grabbed the telephone from Dum-

mie's hand. "Nick Gust speaking," he said. "Yes— no—
What? I don't think I've understood. What did you say?
Really? Wants to take it now? Yes. No. I— Yes, of
course. That's fine. And the money? ... OK, well, thanks
very much." He put the phone back down, shook his
head, scratched his chin and plopped down into his red
chair.

"What's happened?" Angus asked, concerned.

"Something crazy. Something quite extraordinary.
Something—"

"Tell us then," Angus insisted.

"The painting's sold," Nick said.

"You sold a painting? Dad! That's fantastic!"

"No, not me, Dummie. Someone bought Dummie's
painting."

"What? But that one was ten thousand euros!"

"Quite right," Nick said. "Ten thousand euros. The
buyer has paid up and is taking it with him."

Dummie jumped up. "Ghe takes painting? Where?"

"Home, I guess," Nick said. Then a broad smile
appeared on his face. "Dummie! Your painting has
been sold! Now we've got ten thousand eur–" He shut
his mouth and looked at Dummie's furious face.
Dummie's golden eyes were spewing fire and his brown
teeth were clenched. "You said no one want for so much
money!" he screamed.

"Yes, that's what I thought," Nick said, taken aback.
"Aren't you pleased?"

"No! I want back!"

"Then just paint a new one. We've got ten thousand
euros now. That's ten times one thousand!"

"So what. Painting was of my ghome! I want to ghang it, my ghome on my wall!"

"Hmm," Nick said. He scratched his chin. "But that money... do you realize all the things we could do with it?"

"Is money for me?" Dummie asked.

"No. For all of us. That's the way we do things here."

Dummie's eyes became fiercer and he clenched his fists.

"But..." Nick added hastily, "since you painted it, you can choose a present for yourself. Pick anything you want, is that alright?"

Dummie was quiet for a moment. "So I can choose everything?" he asked.

"If it's not too expensive," Nick said. "Well?"

Dummie looked outside. All of sudden a smile appeared on his face. "I know what I want," he said.

"Phew," said Nick. "Tell us and we'll buy it. And after that you must make more paintings and sell them. Dummie, we're going to be rich! Alright, so what do you want?"

"I want to gho to my country," Dummie said decisively.

"What?'

"To Egypt. I want to gho back. Is my ghome."

"Back to Egypt?" Nick and Angus looked at each other in shock.

"I want to see. When can we gho?"

"Well, erm... we can't," Nick said. "We can't go to your country, it's not possible."

"Cannot?" Now Dummie was furious. "You said I

choose!" he screamed. "I choose my country. Is my money!"

"Yes, well. We can't go to Egypt," Nick said.

"Why not?"

"Because... because we can't."

Dummie jumped up so wildly that his chair toppled backwards. "SIR SAR!" he cried, thumping his fist on the table. "You lie. I can choose, but now not. You are mean wuss!"

He ran out of the room, slamming the door behind him.

Nick looked at Angus apologetically. "Ah well," he said.

"He's right, Dad," Angus said. "You did say he could choose."

"But a trip to Egypt. That's much too dangerous, isn't it? They'd see he was a mummy. If there's any place they know about mummies, it's Egypt."

"He doesn't look like a mummy now he's got clean bandages."

"No. Yes. But, erm... He doesn't have a passport!" Nick suddenly seemed a little relieved.

"No passport? I think you're just too scared," Angus said.

"Maybe. But the passport is the trickiest thing. How can you travel without a passport?"

"Do you think I know the answer to that?"

"No. And I don't either," Nick said. "And we don't have passports either, by the way."

"But we could get them."

"Yes, but he couldn't."

Upstairs there was a bang. And another one.

"Whumpy dumpman, he's seriously angry," Nick said. "Go up to him, will you?"

Angus went upstairs. Dummie was standing on his bed and beating his fists very hard on Angus' desk.

"Hey, stop that!" Angus cried. "That must hurt!"

"I feel nothing. Your father is liar!" Dummie snarled.

"He's not. Stop! You'll break something!"

Dummie gave the desk another whack and then plopped down onto the bed with a twisted face.

Angus sat down next to him. "Why do you want to go to Egypt all of a sudden?" he asked.

"Not all of a sudden. I want to gho long time," Dummie said.

"Really? Why didn't you say so earlier?"

"Because Nick ghave no money. But now ghe does. I

make painting, Nick says money for all of us. I am all of us. Nick says I can choose. I choose my country."

"But it's not possible. You don't have a passport," Angus said.

"What is passport?"

"It's a kind of little book. Inside it says who you are. And which country you are from. There's also a photo, as proof that it's really you."

"I am me. I am Dummie," Dummie said angrily.

"Yes, but you don't have a passport. And without a passport you can't travel. You need to have one of those little books to get through customs."

"What is customs?"

"It's someone at the border who says whether the government will let you into a country of not. You have to do what they say."

"Of course I can gho in! Is my country!" Dummie said indignantly. "My father is pharaoh Akhnetut. That is much bigger boss!'

Angus said nothing. When you thought about it, it was pretty complicated.

The door opened and Nick came in. Dummie turned his back on him right away. Nick sat down on Angus' bed and looked uneasily at Dummie's back.

"Dummie, I want to explain something to you," he said. "I get that you want to go back home. Going to Egypt would be the best present you could choose. But it's simply not possible. We can't travel with a mummy."

"I am not mummy. I am burned boy from Egypt," snarled Dummie.

"Yes, that's what we told everyone. And it's going well. No one has realized you are a mummy so far. But it has to stay that way. It's too dangerous. But there's something even more important: you don't have a passport. You can't go abroad without a passport."

"Then we buy little book," Dummie said.

"We can't. You can only buy a passport here if you are a Dutch person. You need a name and an address. And a photo of your face."

Dummie jumped up. "I ghave name and address. I live here. You make photo of bandages!"

Nick shook his head. "Dummie, the answer is no."

"You say no?" Dummie balled his fists and walked up to Nick.

"Stop! Wait a minute!" Angus said hastily. "Erm, what about if we borrow a passport from someone? Ebbi Zanusi, for example, he visits his family in Africa every year. Ebbi's the same age and about the same size as Dummie. That would be alright, wouldn't it, Dad?'

But his father shook his head. "People don't lend out their passports. It's against the law to do so. And everyone thinks that Dummie is my burned nephew from Egypt. He'd have his own passport then, wouldn't he? Otherwise how would he have gotten here? And stop coming up with ideas: we're not going to hide him in a suitcase and we're not going to wrap him up and mail him either." Nick got up. "Dummie, I'm sorry to have to say this but some things are possible and some things aren't. And this isn't."

Dummie stared furiously at Nick. "SIRSAR!" he hissed.

Nick blushed. "Stop it," he said. He turned on his heels and left the room shaking his head.

Dummie lay down on his bed. He took his scarab out from under his bandages and swung it back and forth above his face. Angus looked at his gruesome face with its dried-out skin and the hole where his nose had once been.

"What would you actually want to do in Egypt?" he asked gently.

Dummie closed his eyes. "I ghave same dream, from when I lived there. First not, but now I do. I ghave same dream almost every night."

"Every night? You haven't mentioned it at all."

"Because you don't ask," Dummie said.

Angus was silent. His best friend dreamed of Egypt every night and he knew nothing about it. Was that why Dummie looked so sad at times?

"What happens in your dream then?" he asked.

"I sit on donkey, in line for funeral. Everyone crying. I gho on long road to pyramid. But in dream is also village, with other people. And Ghepsetsut. But when I wake up, I forget. I want to gho there. Maybe then I remember. I want to gho back. I want—" He stopped and bit his torn lip. He looked very sorry for himself.

"What do you want?" Angus insisted.

"I want to gho to Mum and Dad," Dummie whispered.

Angus was startled. He started to feel hot. He hadn't seen this coming. Dummie didn't just want to go to Egypt on a whim, he missed his mum and dad! But they'd been dead for four thousand years! "Dummie, your mum and dad... they aren't there anymore. You know that, don't you?"

"Yes. I know. But I want to gho to ghrave. I want to see."

"But... your father's grave, we don't even know where it is," Angus said.

All of sudden Dummie looked cross. "I find it. I must. I gho back in my country. I ghet there. Your dad is stupid wuss."

"He isn't."

"He is."

Angus looked at Dummie's stubborn face.

Then something awful occurred to him. He had once felt homesick when he was staying at Ebbi's house when he was younger. All he'd wanted was to go home and he'd cried and cried until Nick came to fetch him. And Dummie was even more stubborn than he was. Perhaps Dummie had been waiting until they had some money. But now that they had enough money, he really wanted to go. And if they didn't go with him, maybe he'd go on his own! Then one morning he might suddenly be gone, just the way he'd suddenly appeared. Now Angus was certain that nobody could stop Dummie.

"Dummie, listen. You can't leave us," he insisted. "You live here now. Dad takes care of you. I'm your friend. And you've got other friends at school. You don't know anyone in Egypt."

Dummie said nothing and clenched the scarab even tighter in his hand.

Blasting cackdingle! They'd better make sure Dummie got a passport. And Angus had to keep an eye on Dummie at all times.

"Do you want to play chess?" he asked.

"No."

"Something else?"

Dummie didn't reply and pulled the covers over his head.

Angus decided to stay upstairs for the rest of the evening. He got a book and lay down on his bed. From time to time he looked across at Dummie. After a while Dummie began to snore quietly. Angus silently slipped out of bed and went downstairs. His father was sitting in his red chair staring into space. When he heard Angus, he looked up. "We really can't go to Egypt, you know," he said apologetically.

"He doesn't just want to go to Egypt, he wants to go to his father's grave," Angus said.

"Huh?"

"That's what he's been dreaming about. He dreams of a kind of funeral procession he's walking in. He thinks it's got something to do with his father's grave. He's dead set on going there. I think he's feeling sad."

Nick let out a deep sigh. "Just what we need," he muttered. "He's suffering from homesickness."

"What do we do now then?" Angus asked.

"It doesn't change anything," Nick replied. "We simply can't go there."

"But feeling homesick, that's awful. Do you remember when I got homesick once when I was staying at Ebbi's house? You came to get me because homesickness was really awful, you said."

Nick gave him a serious look. "Angus, Dummie's homesickness is impossible to cure. If you sleep over at Ebbi's and you feel homesick, you can simply go home. But Dummie is missing something that no longer exists. He can't go back in time; no one can. Everything has changed. It's four thousand years later. There aren't any pharaohs anymore, no palaces, nothing. Everything has gone or is buried in the sand. Imagine we did go to Egypt, he'd be thinking he was going home. But his home is no longer there. He'd have such a shock. And about that grave... We'd never find it. Archeologists have spent centuries looking for those things. Very occasionally they'll find a grave, one that was emptied years before. Imagine, Angus, us finding his dad's grave and discovering it has been looted by thieves. Wouldn't that be horrible?"

Angus said nothing. His dad was right of course. But try telling that to Dummie. "Dad, there's something else," he said.

"What is it?"

"I'm frightened," Angus said. "Dummie is so stubborn."

"Yes, tell me about it," Nick said. "He's more stubborn than those three donkeys in the painting put together. But that doesn't mean he has to get his own way."

"Maybe it does. If we don't go, I think he may go by himself. He'll suddenly disappear. We have to look after him. He's all on his own. Maybe his homesickness will be cured when he sees that his Egypt no longer exists. That's possible, isn't it, Dad? That would be good, wouldn't it?'

"Yes, that would be good," Nick admitted. "But that passport is a real problem. I wouldn't know how to get him out of the country. Would you? You're not even allowed to just take along pets when you travel. They need a special letter saying they're healthy. And Dummie isn't just unhealthy, he's dead."

Angus looked at the worry lines on his father's face. If his dad didn't know what to do, how could he solve this? If only that painting had never been sold. Then they wouldn't have any money, and there would be no argument. Now there was ten thousand euros and it wasn't even making anyone happy.

"Mr Scribble might have an idea," Angus suddenly thought. "He knows more than you do."

"No," Nick said. "Angus, I don't want to get on an airplane with a mummy. I just know it would go wrong."

"And I just know Dummie will go on his own otherwise," Angus said. "I'm going to ask Mr Scribble tomorrow. He's the only person who knows that Dummie is a mummy and he always knows everything. He'll help us."

"Angus, it's not what I want," Nick said.

"But it's what Dummie wants," Angus said.

Nick sighed. "I'll talk you out of it tomorrow," he said. "Get to bed now. Night night."

Angus left the room. When he got upstairs he found Dummie sitting bolt upright in bed just staring. "Dummie," Angus whispered. "What's the matter? Did you have that dream again?"

"Yes," Dummie murmured. "I have to gho there."

Angus got into bed. "We'll go and see Mr Scribble tomorrow. He'll be able to help us," he said.

The next day was Sunday. Just like every morning Dummie stank of dead mice and Angus sprayed him with toilet freshener. Then they went downstairs together. To Angus' distress, Dummie and his dad got into an argument immediately.

"Good morning," Nick said.

"I am angry," Dummie said. "I don't speak to you."

"Well, I will speak to you. Did you sleep well?"

"Ghave you thought for passport?"

"No."

"Then you are stupid wuss!"

"Dummie, stop swearing," Nick said sternly. "It's alright to be angry sometimes but not for this long. Today's a new day and we'll start again from scratch."

"I want to gho to Egypt," Dummie said.

"You can't."

"Then I am angry again," Dummie said.

"Oh really. And tomorrow?"

"Tomorrow angry from scratch. You are enemy."

"Enemy?" Nick blushed. "Listen to me, you hothead, you've been living with us for three months now. I've done everything for you. And if I hadn't, you'd be in some research laboratory with your skull sawn open. I've made sure you can go to school and we got your scarab back for you, otherwise you'd be dead. So, will you please stop?"

"No. I am angry," Dummie said.

"Well, I can't just conjure up a passport for you!"

"I want to gho to Egypt," Dummie said.

"You're too much!" Nick stuffed the last bite of toast into his mouth, got up and ran to his workshop. Angus felt sorry for him. His father couldn't do anything about it. But Dummie couldn't either. They really had to go see their teacher. He quickly cleared the table.

"Come on, we're going to see Mr Scribble," he said.

"Ghe make passport for me?" Dummie asked.

"Maybe. Come on!"

They got on their bikes and cycled to the village.

"Hello Dummie, hello Angus, come in," Mr Scribble said. He was still wearing his pyjamas and his hair was sticking up all over the place. "Why have you come so early on a Sunday morning? Is there a problem?"

Angus told him that Dummie had sold a painting for ten thousand euros the night before and that he wanted to go to Egypt. "Dummie wants to visit his father's grave. Dad says he can't because Dummie doesn't have a passport. Dad doesn't want to secretly borrow a passport and he doesn't want to get a fake one. But you always know everything. How can Dummie get a passport?"

Mr Scribble sat down in his chair and frowned. "Usually you go to the town hall and they order one for you. And if you're a foreigner you have to go to the consulate."

"What's that?"

"It's a piece of Egypt in Holland."

"Does it ghave pyramid?" Dummie asked.

"No. It's just a building. It's a bit complicated to explain. But they don't just give you a passport. You have to have lost your old one. Or it got burned or something."

Dummie looked up. "If someone loses passport ghe ghet new one?" he asked. "So say I lost it."

"No, I mean real people. But you're not one. You don't really exist," Mr Scribble said.

"Don't you have another idea?" Angus asked.

Mr Scribble shook his head. When it came to passports he wasn't much cleverer than his dad, Angus thought.

"What should we do?" he asked.

"I'll give you some new books about Egypt," said Mr Scribble. "Then you might be able to see where your father—"

"SIR SAR!" Dummie jumped up. "You are scared wuss! You don't want me to gho to Egypt. You are scared I not come back!" He barged his way to the door and slammed it behind him.

"Now, now," Mr Scribble said in shock.

"He did that at home too," Angus said. "He's suddenly got his heart set on going there. If we don't help him, he'll just go on his own."

"Yeah, I guess he might," Mr Scribble said, concerned.

"So we have to stop him, don't we? I can't let him out of my sight. So I'll have to be with him at all times. But... that's never going to work, is it?" Angus gave Mr Scribble a pleading look. "It's half term in a couple of weeks. We could go then. He just needs a passport. Are you sure you can't come up with a plan?"

"I don't know. Maybe. I'll have a think," Mr Scribble promised. "Hurry after him now, otherwise you'll have lost him already."

Already? Blasting cackdingle! "Alright, I'm off," Angus said hastily.

He ran outside, jumped onto his bike and raced home. Luckily Dummie's bike was already in their garden. But when he got off, he saw Dummie coming out of the house.

"Where are you going?" Angus asked, worried.

"I don't want to see Nick. I'm ghoing to Ebbi," Dummie said.

"OK, I'll come with you," Angus said.

They cycled back to the village together.

"Hey Dummie. Don't worry. Mr Scribble is going to think about the passport. He says he can figure it out," Angus lied.

"Doesn't ghave to. I ghave idea," Dummie said.

"What is it?"

"I make passport. I can draw. I can look at Ebbi's passport through thick ghlass and I copy it."

"Thick glass?"

"That makes bigger, then I see everything."

"Oh, a magnifying glass. Right, well, good." Angus didn't say anything else. Drawing a passport was a silly idea. But at least it would keep Dummie busy for a while and in the meantime Mr Scribble would have a chance to come up with something.

As they rested their bikes against Ebbi's house, Ebbi's head appeared out of his bedroom window.

"Hi Angus, hi Dummie," Ebbi cried cheerfully. "The back door's open!"

Angus and Dummie walked round the back and went up the stairs.

"Where are your mum and dad?" Dummie asked.

"Gone for coffee somewhere. Shall we play soccer?"

"Yes, soon. I ghave question first. Do you ghave passport?"

Ebbi looked surprised. "Of course," he said. "We go to

visit relatives in Africa each year. You can't go without one. Why?"

"Can I see it?" Dummie asked.

"Why?"

"Because I never seen one."

"Don't you have your own passport? How did you get into the country otherwise?"

"His passport looks different," Angus blurted out. "It's Egyptian. He just wants to know what a Dutch passport looks like. But I don't have one."

Luckily Ebbi didn't keep asking questions. "Alright then. Wait a sec."

Ebbi disappeared and returned with a dark red little book.

Dummie studied it from every angle. Then he got a magnifying glass out of his pocket and opened the passport.

"You look like a detective with that thing," Ebbi giggled. "Are you looking for fingerprints?"

"Just looking," Dummie said vaguely.

He studied each page attentively. Finally he closed the passport.

"Are we going to play soccer now?" Ebbi asked impatiently.

"Yes, in field," Dummie said. "Coming?"

They left the things on Ebbi's desk and went outside. Angus breathed a deep sigh of relief. For a moment he'd expected Dummie to run off with Ebbi's passport. But it seemed as though he had just wanted to see it. Strange though, couldn't Dummie see that he wouldn't be able to just copy it?

They walked to the field and started to play football. From time to time Dummie glanced at Ebbi's house. Maybe he was still plotting something Angus thought. But what? Dummie looked at the house again and suddenly kicked the ball really hard past the goal. The ball flew over the ditch and landed a long way off in a meadow.

"I'll get it!" Angus cried. He took a long run up, jumped over the ditch and ran to get the ball.

When he returned, Dummie had gone. "Where's Dummie?" he asked, concerned.

"Just gone for a pee," Ebbi said.

A pee? Dummie didn't need to pee because he didn't have a stomach anymore and he never ate or drank! Angus looked at the house and almost jumped out of his skin. There was a trail of smoke coming from Ebbi's window. "Ebbi! Fire!" he shouted.

They ran back to Ebbi's house as fast as they could.

"Dummie! Dummie!"

They could smell burning from the kitchen. At that same instant, Angus heard Dummie scream.

He raced up the stairs to Ebbi's bedroom. To his

dismay, the bin next to Ebbi's desk was on fire and there were flames on Dummie's bandages. Angus didn't hesitate, he ran to the bathroom and filled a glass with water. He threw it over Dummie in one fluid movement. Dummie began to scream even louder. "Not water! Otherwise I dissolve!"

"Otherwise you'll burn!"

The fire on Dummie was out. But in the meantime the bin had turned into a small bonfire. To make matters worse, Dummie knocked a pile of magazines into it.

"Look out!" Angus shouted. He quickly looked around. He needed a bucket. In the bathroom! There was a big bin there! He ran back, tipped out the contents of the bin and turned the tap on full. Ten seconds later he was emptying the whole lot onto the flames. There was a hiss and a dark cloud of smoke rose to the ceiling.

"It's out," Angus panted.

"Mary and Moses," Ebbi muttered. "How could this happen?"

"I come for toilet. I smell fire," groaned Dummie. "I run up, I see fire on desk. I throw fire on bin. But bin burns worse. I am scared."

"Unlike me," Ebbi said sarcastically. "What was on fire then?"

"Ebbi?" came the voice of Ebbi's mother. "Ebbi? Are you there? I can smell burning!"

There were hurried footsteps on the stairs and Mrs Zanusi came running in.

"My lord, what on earth has happened here?"

"Fire was ghere! I ghave put out!" Dummie said, clutching his arm.

"But how did the fire start? Were you playing with fire? What's the matter with your arm?"

"Wet. Oh, no, is my fault!" Dummie moaned. "I put thick ghlass! Thick ghlass was on passport on desk in sun. Mr Scribble tell us about fire making. It is danger-ous. I forget. I did it!"

"Passport? Is your passport burnt, Ebbi? What was your passport doing here?"

"I wanted to see," Dummie said guiltily. "Stupid. But lucky, I ghave idea. Ebbi can ghet new passport."

Angus looked at Dummie in confusion. Mr Scribble had indeed taught them that you could start a fire with a magnifying glass. Had Dummie done it deliberately so that Ebbi could get a new passport? But how was that going to help Dummie? He'd almost burned himself! And his arm was still wet.

"Does it hurt?" Mrs Zanusi asked in concern.

"Water hurts Dummie because of his burns," Ebbi said.

"Should I take the bandage off for you?" Mrs Zanusi asked.

"No," said Angus quickly. "It'll dry on its own."

Mrs Zanusi picked up the bin and looked at the black mush inside it. She lifted out the magnifying glass between her thumb and forefinger. "That's all that's left," she said with a grimace. "Well, we were very fortunate. I'm really happy you had to go to the toilet. If you hadn't come back the whole house might have burned down."

"Thick ghlass was mine," Dummie said guiltily. "And passport is burned."

"Ach, we'll just apply for a new one," said Mrs Zanusi. "I'm just glad nothing worse happened."

"I am very ghood," Dummie said, suddenly grinning proudly.

They went downstairs and Ebbi's mother gave Dummie a big bag of sweets. "You two just go home," she said. "I'll clear up the mess."

"Thank you. I like," Dummie said smugly.

Angus couldn't believe his ears. That boy was really disturbed.

They waved and got onto their bikes.

"I don't understand you at all," Angus said crossly as they cycled out of the village. "Did you light a fire on purpose?"

"Yes, I did it," Dummie said. "Was ghood idea."

"It wasn't a good idea at all! The whole house could have gone up in flames!"

"But it didn't gho in flames. Mr Scribble said you could ghet a new passport if it ghet burned. Ebbi will ghet new passport."

"So what? It still doesn't give you a passport, does it?"

"Oh no?" Dummie got down, took something out of his bandages and handed it to Angus.

Angus stared at the dark red book in astonishment. Blasting cackdingle! It was Ebbi's passport! Now Angus felt like slapping his forehead. Dummie was much cleverer than he'd thought. He didn't want to copy Ebbi's passport at all, nor did he want to steal it. He wanted to make everyone think that Ebbi's passport had burned. No one would ask any questions then.

"Ebbi ghets new one. This one for me," Dummie said proudly. "Is ghood idea, no?"

"Yes. No. You're totally crazy!" Angus bristled. "What do you think my dad will say?"

"Nick is ghappy. Now we can gho to Egypt," Dummie said.

Angus said nothing. Nick happy? His father was going to be very angry.

Dummie threw his bike down in the garden and walked around to the back of the house. Nick was painting in the shed. "Did you have a nice time playing outside?" he asked. Then he saw the black splotch on Dummie's bandage. "What happened to you?" he asked, shocked.

"Ghere," said Dummie. He held out the passport to Nick and gave him a triumphant look.

"What's that?"

"Passport. For me."

Nick wiped his hands, took the passport and opened it. "This is Ebbi's passport," he cried in amazement. "How did you get it?"

Angus bowed his head and told him that Dummie had started a fire with a magnifying glass and pretended that Ebbi's passport had got burned. "But nothing bad happened. It was only the waste paper basket that got burned."

"What?!" Nick was furious. "Are you out of your minds!" he shouted. "Stealing a passport! If anyone finds out... You have to take it back at once!"

"Can't," Dummie said. "Is burned. We are ghoing to Egypt?"

"No!"

"No?" Dummie exploded. He charged at Nick with his fists balled and grabbed at the passport.

But Nick wouldn't let go. "Stop it! Getting angry won't help. I don't care if you bring all of Polderdam running with your screams." He picked up Dummie, put him outside the shed and locked the door. As Dummie banged on the door, he turned around and picked up a pair of scissors.

"What are you doing?" Angus asked, aghast.

"I'm going to cut it up," Nick growled. "If anyone sees it, we could get arrested."

"Don't do it! Stop! Whaah!" screamed Angus.

Nick lowered the scissors. "Whumpy dumpman! What's wrong with the two of you?"

All of a sudden Angus felt angry. "Nothing's wrong with us! Something's wrong with you! Don't you remember that Dummie almost died? Then we stole the scarab back and that was wrong too. But we did it anyway because nothing was normal anymore. Things will never be normal again with Dummie here. We've got the only living mummy in the world staying in our house and he wants to go home. And now we've got money and a passport and you don't even dare because you're afraid Dummie will be found out. Have you forgotten what you always say? You see what you think you're seeing. So no one sees that Dummie's a mummy. And they won't in Egypt either. Dummie's right. You're a stupid wuss!" Then Angus closed his mouth in fright and looked at his father. He could say anything to his dad, they'd agreed on that. But not like this. He didn't usually say this kind of thing. See that everything had stopped being normal?

He turned around and walked toward the door which Dummie was still banging on. His hand was on the door handle when Nick called out to him.

"Stop. Wait. Angus!"

Angus stopped. Now he was getting his punishment. Maybe he'd be grounded for a week. Or a month of no television. But to his surprise, Nick said something crazy. He said, "You're right. I am a stupid wuss."

"Huh?"

"An incredibly stupid wuss.'

"Yes. No. Of course not," said Angus in confusion. "What do you mean?"

"Well... because I'm scared of flying," Nick said.

Angus' jaw dropped. "What? Is that why you don't want to go to Egypt?"

"No. But I've just thought of it. Nothing is normal anymore. So this isn't either. We're going to Egypt."

Angus blinked several times. Blasting cackdingle.

Getting angry did help sometimes!

He opened the door and Dummie almost flew at Nick. It was a while before he understood that Nick had changed his mind and when he did, his tantrum stopped immediately.

"Ghooray! Ghooray!" he cried. "You are ghood."

"Yes, out of my good mind," Nick muttered.

They went into the house, Nick turned on the computer and half an hour later he'd booked three airplane tickets and a hotel room. As he printed everything, he kept on muttering, "I probably need my head seeing to. How is this going to work? What am I thinking?" and that kind of thing. He took the papers from the printer, held them up in the air and looked at them as though he'd just booked a one-way ticket to the moon.

"Come on, Dad, we're only going to Egypt," Angus said.

"Yes. With a mummy and a burned passport," Nick said. "It's giving me terrible stomach cramps. And I'm terrified."

"That'll pass when we're eating our pizzas," Angus grinned.

"Which pizzas?"

"The ones we're about to make. We've got something to celebrate, haven't we?"

So Nick made pizzas that evening and he burned them for the first time in his life. He was totally preoccupied and worried. As they sat picking off the burnt bits of crust, Dummie smiled away. "We're ghoing to my ghome! Ghooray! You are very ghood!" he said to Nick.

"Yes, yes. And this morning I was a stupid wuss," Nick muttered.

"But now not. Maybe tomorrow again," Dummie said cheerfully.

"You can get that out of your head. Tomorrow we're going to buy new clothes and sort out passports for ourselves. And we'll practice every single evening. From Saturday onwards you'll no longer be Dummie but the burned Dutch boy Ebbi."

"MAASHI. I am burned Dutch Ebbi."

"And your last name."

"Ebbi Zanusi. I am ten years. I gho to Egypt to my father's ghrave."

"No, you mustn't say that. We've not going to a grave. We're just going on holiday. Say you're not going to do anything there," Nick said.

"Nothing? No one will believe that. Then better not to gho."

"Dummie, it will be packed with people not doing anything on holiday."

"Really? People are crazy. Waste of journey. I am not crazy."

"Whumpy dumpman, that's not the point," Nick said crossly. "You're not going to a grave!"

Angus burst out laughing. "Dummie's not wrong, Dad. Everyone in Egypt goes to see graves, it's crazy if you don't."

"I don't understand. So I gho to ghrave or not to ghrave?" Dummie asked.

Nick rolled his eyes. "Alright then, you're going to a grave. But not your father's grave," he finished.

"Ghood. I gho to any old ghrave," Dummie said.

Angus could hardly control his giggles and pulled Dummie outside with him before his father could stop them. "We're going to play soccer, Dad. Why don't you sit in your red chair until you feel better again."

"Huh?"

"Bye!"

When they went back him, Nick had made a list of the things they should take with them. Dummie and Angus went to bed.

"You have to be extra nice to my father from now on," Angus said when they were lying under their covers. "He's scared of flying."

"What? We are ghoing flying?" Dummie asked in disbelief. "Can't be."

"We're not, but the airplane will. It's erm... a kind of car in the sky, with wings."

"Flying donkey," said Dummie.

"Something like that," Angus grinned. "My dad finds it scary. Shh, he's coming."

Nick came in and sat down on Dummie's bed. "What's your name again?" he asked.

"Darwishi ur-Atum Msamaki Minkabh Ishaq Eboni," Dummie replied.

"Whumpy dumpman! Have you forgotten already? You're called Ebbi!" shouted Nick.

"What you mean? Is it Saturday?"

"No. We just have to practice!"

"I remember. Saturday I am Ebbi Zanusi. Saturday we don't gho to my father's ghrave. I'm not ghoing to do anything. Is not a waste of journey. And not scary in flying donkey."

Angus burst out laughing again and even Nick had to laugh then. "Exactly," he said. "Night night."

The next day they got to school extra early. Mr Scribble was already in the classroom.

"Hello Angus, hello Dummie. Everything alright?"

"Ghood," said Dummie. "You don't have to think about passport."

"Great," Mr Scribble said in relief. "I really couldn't think of anything. So do you want to borrow some books about Egypt?"

"No. We're ghoing to my country. I ghave passport," Dummie said.

"What?"

Angus quickly told him about the fire in Ebbi's house, and how Ebbi's passport had got 'burned'. "My father already booked the tickets."

Dummie grinned. "You say person ghet new passport if old book is burned. I did with thick ghlass. You told me, you know," he said.

"Oh," said Mr Scribble sheepishly. "I'm teaching you the wrong things, it seems. Erm... Did I also tell you to set fire to someone's house?"

"No. You said: use thick ghlass in emergency. This is emergency."

Mr Scribble shook his head. "Well, you remembered that very well. " Then he turned around and Angus saw him repressing a laugh. "And when are you leaving?"

"Saturday. Beginning of holiday."

"Alright. That's good. I will see if I can help you in any way."

Then the school bell went.

After school they went into town to buy new clothes. They bought three pairs of white trousers to wear in the heat and three big straw hats to prevent them from getting sunstroke. They got some Egyptian money and a suitcase. And they borrowed a second suitcase from Mr Scribble.

Nick sat down on Dummie's bed every night to practice and every night Dummie said he wouldn't be called Ebbi until Saturday, after which Nick went back downstairs shaking his head.

In the meantime, they had to go to school as usual. Dummie told everyone every day that he was going back home on Saturday. One time he climbed to the top of the climbing frame during the break and shouted out over the playground, "I'm ghoing ghome! MAASHI! Ghooray!"

All of the children had to laugh at Dummie, except for Annalisa. Annalisa hadn't liked Dummie ever since he'd started at the school because he smelled and he looked funny.

"So you're finally going back?" she said, cattily.

"Gholiday, in desert."

Annalisa laughed in his face. "Holiday in the desert, ha ha ha. We're going to the seaside, swimming in the sea. Now that's a real holiday."

"My country is better," Dummie said.

"Great, then you'll stay there then? At last!" Annalisa said spitefully. "Maybe your mum and dad are better by now. Then you can stay there. As a mummy."

But Dummie was much too excited to let that stupid Annalisa wind him up. "Maybe you get eaten by shark. Then you stay too," he said happily. "As shark poop."

Ebbi almost choked with laughter. Annalisa turned red and shut her mouth.

"You are coming back afterwards, aren't you?" Ebbi asked when he'd stopped laughing.

Angus shot Dummie a glance. Actually, Ebbi was asking what he was afraid of himself.

"Yes. Is just gholiday. I gho to do nothing," Dummie said.

"Phew," Ebbi said.

Hmm, Angus thought.

On Thursday evening, Mr Scribble turned up at their house with a book filled with notes. In the months that Dummie had been at the school, he'd told them a few things about the past, and Mr Scribble had noted it all down.

"According to the museum you were in, you are from the fifth or sixth dynasty, which is about 4,200 years ago, and you were found near Gizeh," he began. "That was called Sakkara before. It was the place the old Egyptians used to bury their kings. And your palace would have been in the old capital of Memphis because all of the pharaohs lived there at that time. But unfortunately there's nothing left of that."

"And Gizeh then? He said that name once," Angus asked.

"That's not too far away," Mr Scribble said. "A couple of enormous pyramids were built there just before his time. I'm sure he would have seen them and he'll remember them. They were a great wonder, they were so massive."

Angus nodded. That sounded logical.

"Good. And about your father," Mr Scribble began. "Your father was called Akhnetut, you said. I have managed to find that name. There is an unknown pharaoh from the sixth dynasty who was probably called Akhnetut. So he must have been buried in Sakkara. But his grave has never been found."

"Alright. Then we'll have to head for that city," Angus said.

"Sakkara isn't a city. It's an enormous burial site in the desert. But to be honest, there's not much left of that either."

"But the pyramids are still there, aren't they?" Angus asked.

Mr Scribble nodded. "There's even the oldest pyramid in Egypt in Sakkara. But there's a problem. The Akhnetut I found only reigned for two years. He probably died very young, right after Dummie. Perhaps from the same illness. And so Akhnetut doesn't have a pyramid of his own."

"No pyramid? Why not?" Angus asked in surprise.

"Because they were built while the pharaohs were still alive. If a pharaoh died before the pyramid was finished, they simply stopped building it. Perhaps they hadn't even started. So Dummie's father will be in a small grave somewhere. A simple tomb under the ground, I think." He looked even more serious. "Dummie, people look for graves in Sakkara almost every day, archeologists – people who have studied how to find them. And they only rarely find graves. The chance of you finding your father's grave is actually..."

"I find it," Dummie interrupted him.

Alright," Mr Scribble said. Angus looked at his face. Mr Scribble didn't think it would be alright at all. And neither did Angus. A small tomb under the ground, it could be anywhere!

"Have you got any more tips?" he asked. "I mean, what exactly should we look for? And if we find something, how do we know we've found the right one?"

"That's a very good question," said Mr Scribble. "And luckily I have the answer." He pulled a piece of cardboard with a drawing on it from his notebook. "Look. This is a cartouche. Every pharaoh had his own cartouche. It's a kind of signature in hieroglyphics. This was carved into statues and on the walls of the temples the pharaohs had built. The left their signature behind on everything. And it will certainly be on his grave too. And I think..." he held up the cardboard, "... Akhnetut's cartouche will look something like this. Dummie, have you seen this before?"

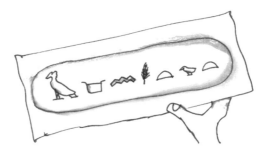

Angus was intrigued and took a close look at the drawing. The cartouche was oval-shaped and contained seven hieroglyphics: a bird, a kind of upside down hat, a zigzag stripe next to a feather, and a chick between two mountains. Dummie grabbed the piece of card from Mr Scribble's hands and began to jump up and down. "I know! This is Akhnetut! Akhnetut! Is from my father!"

Mr Scribble looked at him sheepishly. "Wow, so it really is the right one! Well, you'll have to look for this!" Angus had to laugh at his look of bewilderment. Their teacher was even clever than he realized.

Mr Scribble gave the notebook to Nick. "And there's something else," he added, serious again. "Dummie, I have to warn you. You know that Egypt is very different now than it was four thousand years ago?"

"Yes. Nick said," Dummie replied cheerfully.

"So you'll think you're home, but you might be shocked."

"I won't shock from my ghome. Is nice."

"Dummie, it won't look the same."

"I know. Nice!" Dummie found everything nice. As long as they were still going.

Mr Scribble opened his bag and took out a package. "Right then. So this is for you," he said.

Dummie unwrapped it and took out a camera. "What is this?"

"It's a camera. I want you to take pictures for me." He explained to Dummie how the camera worked and that you could look at the photos you'd taken right away. He took a photo of Dummie and showed it to him. Dummie shrieked. "MAASHI! I am in photo! Nice! Angus, come! We will photo cow!" He didn't wait but ran outside. When Angus went to chase after him, Mr Scribble held him back.

MAASHI!!
I AM iN Photo!

"Nick, Angus, you really won't find the grave, you know," he said with concern. "It's impossible. All the graves there have been plundered or destroyed. They have found the occasional mummy but that's all. Only Tutankhamen's grave was still intact when they discovered it. But that other matter is more important. Dummie probably thinks I'm exaggerating, but it's not just Sakkara and the old capital of Memphis that are gone. Almost everything has gone. Things have been stolen, have sunk into the sand or been destroyed by earthquakes. If you wait long enough, everything disappears. There's nothing left over of his old country. Dummie can't go home, simply because his home is no longer there."

"But isn't Egypt full of temples?" Nick asked.

"Most of them were built after his lifetime," Mr Scribble said.

"What's left from his lifetime then?" Angus asked.

"Ruins. Crumbling pyramids, excavated graves. And the desert."

A horrible feeling washed over Angus. Dummie was happy they were going and he was happy for Dummie. But now... He tried to imagine what it would be like if he returned to Polderdam after four thousand years and everything was different. People would be flying around in spaceships, wearing different clothes and eating different food. It would drive one crazy, wouldn't it?

"Should we really go?" Nick sighed. "He'll only be disappointed."

"You can't change your mind now. Angus is right. He'd only run away otherwise. You are better off going with him. Start by going somewhere that hasn't changed. The big pyramids at Gizeh. He'll know those. You'll see the desert there too. And then go to the museum in Cairo. You can see everything there that has been preserved; statues but also mummies. They've got everything from Tutankhamen's grave. And there are other things they found. Maybe there'll be something there that belonged to Akhnetut. And only after that, you should go to Sakkara and show him what his home looks like now. Let him say goodbye to it. Maybe he'll find that enough. In the meantime, you'll have to take good care of him. You'll have to console him when he doesn't find the grave. And most importantly, bring him back with you. Whatever else happens."

"Of course," Angus and Nick both said at the same time.

"Are you coming?" Dummie asked, poking his head around the door. "Photos is ghood!"

"You can do that tomorrow. You two have to go to bed now," Nick said.

Mr Scribble closed his bag. "One last thing, Dummie. Do you know what a souvenir is? It's something nice that you bring back from another country. Would you please bring something nice back from your country?"

"Of course I can," Dummie said. "Everything nice in my country."

Yes, maybe it was once, Angus thought.

Dummie hurriedly took a picture of Mr Scribble and then they went to bed.

Angus couldn't get to sleep. If Mr Scribble was right, they'd never find the grave. But maybe Dummie would remember something once they were there. That was possible. But if he didn't, then Angus and his dad would be in trouble. What if Dummie refused to leave Egypt until he'd found the grave?

On Friday evening, they wrapped Dummie up in clean bandages and sprayed him with toilet freshener. Angus sewed a new flap for Dummie's face and then Nick also asked him to sew the chain of Dummie's scarab onto the bandages. Dummie couldn't risk losing his scarab again and if he lost it in Egypt, it would be even worse.

Dummie wanted to go to bed straight away because then it would be Saturday sooner, he said.

Angus went upstairs with him. As Dummie fell asleep next him, he had an idea. He got a piece of cardboard and turned it into three small cards of the cartouche, one for each of them. They'd have to carry them with them all the time in Egypt. The door opened quietly and Nick came in. He looked over Angus' shoulder at the drawings.

"That's clever, Angus. I'd forget it otherwise."

He went over to Dummie's bed and stared for a while at his gruesome face. Dummie's mouth was half open and he was snoring.

"Sometimes I wish that Dummie had never come here," he said, suddenly. "I wish he'd walked into someone else's house that day, during that storm. Or that we'd called someone who was more of an expert. You know, sometimes I just can't stop wondering, what if—?"

Angus was shocked. He couldn't imagine life without Dummie now. "Where would we get an expert on living mummies?" he asked. "You just have to think hard, Dad. You always know everything." This wasn't entirely true, and ever since Dummie had turned up on their doorstep, it was as though his Dad knew less and less. "We're doing alright, aren't we?" he asked, anxiously.

"Yeah. We're doing the best we can in any case." Nick stood up. "Well. We'll see. Are you excited about going to Egypt?"

"I'm not sure. I'm afraid it might not be any fun at all," Angus said.

"Me too," said Nick. "And do you know what I'm even more scared of?"

"What?" Angus asked.

"Of flying. Even just thinking about it is giving me diarrhea."

CHAPTER 2

THE Big Trip

That Saturday was one of the worst days of Angus' life.
Flying with his father was a disaster. Nick didn't just
have diarrhea, he was totally useless.

The day started when Mr Scribble rode his bike into
their garden at six o'clock in the morning. Dummie was
standing at the window impatiently, ready sprayed and
wearing his straw hat. "There ghe is! Nice! I gho
ghome! I gho to Egypt! Ghooray!"

Nick opened the door, tripped over a suitcase, fell flat
on his face in the hall and gave himself a nosebleed.

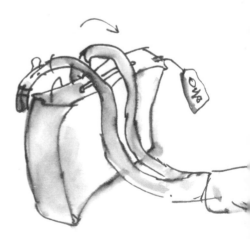

"How did you manage not to notice such a big suitcase?" Angus asked, as he let Mr Scribble in.

"Because I didn't sleep a wink all night," Nick complained, holding a hanky to his nose. "I'm terrified. I've lost my nerve. I don't even know how it works, flying."

Mr Scribble tried to reassure him. He calmly explained that first you have to go to the check-in desk to get your boarding card, then you go through customs, and then you look for the right airplane. "And then you sit down and the pilot does the rest," he said.

"And what if the pilot has a heart attack?" Nick asked, looking panicked.

"Then there's another pilot," Mr Scribble said.

"And what if he has a heart attack too?"

"Then you crash." Mr Scribble winked at Angus.

"Come on, stop it. The only person about to have a heart attack is you."

"Yes," groaned Nick. "I want one!"

"Dad, shut up about flying," Angus said. "You're the grown up, you have to take care of us."

"Yes, I do that all the time! Where's my rucksack?" Nick asked.

"On your back!" Angus didn't say anything else. Mr Scribble winked at him again, but it didn't help. His father was running around like a headless chicken, bleeding all over the place, and then he didn't even help putting the luggage in the car. Angus could only hope he'd find his head again before they had to show their passports.

They drove out of the village and onto the motorway. Just before they reached the airport, a large airplane flew right over their heads. Its wheels were down and the noise was deafening. "Flying donkey!" Dummie cried in excitement.

"Looks more like a dragon with wheels to me," Nick muttered.

"Shut up, Dad!"

Mr Scribble parked in front of the departures hall and got the suitcases out of the boot.

"Listen. You'll have to show your passports a couple of times," he said. "First at the check-in desk, then at customs, and once more when you board the plane. Right, off you go then."

"Yes, off we go then," Nick repeated glumly.

Angus fetched a trolley for their luggage, they waved goodbye to Mr Scribble and went into the departures hall. Nick looked for the right desk on a television screen and not long after that they found themselves in a long queue. Some people gave Dummie a curious look and pointed at him. But Angus no longer worried about that kind of thing, they were used to it by now. Usually they'd whisper something about burns, and everyone felt sorry for Dummie. But what worked best was if you didn't react at all. No, he was much more worried about his father. They had to show their passports three times, so Nick would have to act normal three times. When Angus looked at his red face, it seemed impossible.

"Alright, Dad?"

"No," Nick said. "I'm scared of saying the wrong thing. You have to help me, Angus."

"How? I'm not very good at lying," Angus said. "You are. Can you remember telling everyone at school that Dummie was your Egyptian nephew who was coming to stay with us for a while? You just said it as if you were ordering a sausage roll at the bakery. You're much more imaginative than me."

"Really?"

"Yes. So let's agree on this. Dummie, you just say that you're called Ebbi. And Dad, I'll keep an eye on everything. If you need to lie, I'll say "sausage roll", alright?"

"Anything with it?" his father asked idiotically.

"No, just a plain sausage roll, OK?"

"OK," Nick said.

When it was their turn, Angus kept his eyes and ears open. But to his relief, his father didn't have to lie at all.

The lady at the desk took a good look at Dummie. She compared their passports to the names on the tickets and only asked whether they'd like to sit next to the window. Then they had to put the suitcases onto a conveyor belt and that was that. The lady only started to stare when Dummie climbed onto the conveyor belt too.

"Hey, what are you doing?" she asked in surprise.

"I am Ebbi. I must gho in airplane," Dummie said.

The lady burst out laughing. "No, Ebbi, that's for the baggage compartment. You need to go over there. You take care with all of those bandages, alright? Have a good trip." And then they were allowed to just walk off.

"See, that was easy," Angus said in relief.

Nick didn't look relieved at all. "But the customs people are responsible for passports," he said. "I'm sure they'll look more carefully." He took a couple of deep breaths. "Alright. Here we go." By now his face was redder than a red pepper. He looked very suspicious. If Angus was a customs man, he'd check him six times over. He took his father's arm. "Dad, if you don't hold it together now, I'll be really mad! Do you hear me?"

"Yes, I'm not deaf." Nick went to stand in the next queue with a dazed look on his face, three passports in his hand.

Unfortunately, the customs officer was much more careful. He looked from Dummie to Ebbi's passport and back. "Are you Ebbi Zanusi?" he asked in a stern voice.

Dummie began to speak mechanically, "Yes. I am ten years. I ghave ghad accident. I am burned. I am sad. I gho to Egypt. I do nothing there."

"Yes, yes," the man said. "But can I see your face for a moment?"

"No," Angus said quickly. "He's totally burned."

The man frowned. "How am I supposed to do my job?" he muttered. "I'm sorry, I have to see your face, otherwise it would be easy to smuggle anyone that way."

Angus gave his father a prod. Now it was his turn to speak. But Nick looked as though he totally agreed with the man.

"Sausage roll," Angus hissed.

"Not now. I couldn't get a thing down my throat," Nick whispered.

"I mean: sausage roll! Now! Dad!"

"Oh right, erm..." Nick shook his head and cleared his throat. "Listen, sir," he began in a deep voice. "If I wanted to secretly smuggle someone I'd hide them in a suitcase. But fine, if you insist on seeing his face, you'll just have to. But I must warn you. It's ulcerated and festering and he looks like he belongs in a haunted house."

The officer raised his eyebrows. "A haunted house?"

"You know, at the fun fair. The skin's hanging off. It's really horrible to look at. I mean, there's almost no face left."

Angus closed his eyes. Now his father was saying too much.

"What do you mean exactly?" the man asked suspiciously.

"My father's exaggerating a bit," Angus said quickly. "But you really can't see his face. He has to stay wrapped up. Otherwise bacteria will get in. My dad was just joking."

"I am Ebbi Zaunusi," Dummie repeated.

The man hesitated.

Suddenly someone began to complain. "Hey, how long's this going to take? Does that burned kid look like a criminal? A mummy, more like."

Angus turned around. Behind them, a big fat man was rocking impatiently on his heels.

The customs officer shook his head and reluctantly closed Ebbi's passport. "Right. Have fun in Egypt then. I hope your mummy doesn't get too hot there."

"Oh, he's used to it," Nick said. "Come on, boys. Goodbye, sir."

And then they were through customs and they'd managed it.

"Pff," Angus said. "You can say really stupid things sometimes, Dad. And why are you walking so fast?"

"I'm desperate for the loo," groaned Nick.

They hurried on. But before they arrived at the toilets there was another queue.

Curious, Angus watched what was happening. All the people were taking off their belts and these were disappearing along with their bags into a kind of box above a conveyor belt. Then they had to walk through a door and if the door began to beep, they were frisked by a stern guard in a uniform.

"What's that, Dad?"

"Security," Nick said. "They're looking for metal. They check if anyone's got a gun. Or maybe a bomb. Well, come on. Take everything off."

He put his rucksack on the conveyor belt, took off his belt and walked through the door without it beeping.

Angus pushed Dummie ahead of him. "Don't say anything, just walk through," he whispered.

Dummie hesitated and tiptoed towards the door. No sooner had he gone through it when something began to beep very loudly. "Whaah!" cried Dummie and he darted back. Angus nearly died of fright.

"Have you got something metal on you?" the guard asked sharply.

"No," said Dummie. "I am Ebbi Zanusi. I am burned. I gho..."

"Shh. I know what it is. It's your scarab!" Angus hissed. "Show him your scarab."

"No," said Dummie.

"Yes, you have to show it. You have to!"

Dummie reluctantly pulled the scarab out from under his bandages.

The guard looked at the big golden beetle with suspicion.

"What is it?" he asked.

"Is mine," Dummie said.

"Too big. It has to go through the X-ray machine," the man said. "Put it on the conveyor belt."

"No," said Dummie. "Can't."

"Sorry, sonny, I don't make the rules."

"It's sewn onto his bandages," Angus said quickly. "It's already been stolen once."

"We're not thieves," the man snapped. "Can't he cut it off?"

"No! Is not bomb!"

"Bomb? What kind of bomb?" The guard squinted. "You're pulling my leg, aren't you?"

Angus started to feel hot. "Let him cut it off," he whispered. "Do it, otherwise we'll never get to Egypt!"

"No."

"Yes. It has to go through that box."

"Alright." To Angus' horror Dummie turned around and before he could stop him, he'd climbed onto the conveyor belt and disappeared into the x-ray machine. Soon he was out the other side again. "Ghood now?"

The man who was sitting at the machine could hardly control himself. "Ha ha ha. Never seen that before," he hiccupped.

The miserable guard looked on dumbfounded as Dummie got back down. "Well that's wonderful!" he snorted. "It's not an amusement park, you know! Did you check the scarab?"

"Yes. Didn't see anything. Just bones," the other man laughed. "Let that poor boy go. It's fine now."

Angus hurried through the door now, smiled at the man behind the box and went to his father. Nick was coughing as though he'd just swallowed a wasp.

"Whumpy dumpman. I think I'm having a heart attack."

"Wait until we're in the plane," Angus said. "And look, there's the toilet."

Before they were in the airplane, Nick had to go to the toilet another three times because of his nerves.

Angus couldn't understand how someone could poo that many times in a row. The last time Nick was gone for so long that they were almost late. The lady who was doing the final check quickly let them through. Finally they got onto the airplane.

If Angus thought then that they'd cleared all the obstacles, he was wrong. By now, Nick was so frightened he was a quivering wreck. He was sweating like a horse and he puffed and panted as though he was about to die. Dummie wanted to sit by the window, Angus sat next to him and Nick sunk into the aisle seat.

"Hush now, Dad, the pilot's going to do the rest," Angus said encouragingly.

His father nodded obediently and leaned back. But when a stewardess came to stand in the aisle with a life vest, he sat bolt upright. "What's that? She's going to tell us what we have to do when we crash!" he said fearfully.

"Dad, calm down," Angus said.

"But it's true! If we weren't going to crash, she wouldn't have to tell us what to do!"

"Dad!" Because his father was scared, he was feeling more worried himself. And so was Dummie. He watched the explanation about life vests and emergency exits with slides with a look of mistrust. When the stewardess started telling them what to do if there was smoke any- where, Nick closed his eyes. "Perfect, and now we'll burst into flames in the air to top it all," he muttered.

Angus said nothing and simply gazed outside. The stewardess checked whether all the seat belts were done up properly, the engines started and slowly the airplane taxied to the runway. There was a moment's silence as they paused and then suddenly the engines began to roar. The plane jerked as it accelerated. Faster and faster, until they were going much faster than a car. Suddenly Angus was pressed back in his chair and they flew up into the air. Not long after that, the plane tilted to one side and Angus got a strange feeling in his stomach.

"What ghappen?" Dummie asked, scared.

"My stomach seems to think we're turning," Nick piped up. He was no longer red but as white as Dum- mie's bandages.

"Come on, Dad. For Dummie," Angus whispered.

"What do you mean? He doesn't even have a stom- ach!"

He was right about that. But even though Dummie

couldn't get sick, he could just start to scream. "Whaah! Wrong! Wings broken!"

Angus was startled and looked past Dummie and out the window in panic, but the wings were still whole.

"Look! Wings not flapping! Broken!" Dummie screamed.

Angus almost burst out laughing from the nerves. This was all he needed. And his father still didn't react! Angus was in charge of two little kids.

"The wings of a plane never flap," he said quickly. "It's not a bird."

But Dummie was in a total panic. "I want to ghet out of flying donkey!" he shrieked. To make matters worse, he grabbed the life vest from under his seat, pulled it over his head and blew it up. He unfastened his seatbelt and pointed at the emergency exit, shouting, "There, open it! I want to ghet out of broken bird!"

Angus clamped hold of Dummie and looked around. Everyone was staring at Dummie now, some people with pity but a few were just angry. Dummie tried to break free. "Dad, do something!" Angus cried helplessly.

Suddenly a stewardess appeared next to Nick and whispered something in his ear. Nick nodded, unfasted his seatbelt and stood up.

"Where are you going?" Angus asked, his voice cracking.

"We can move to first class, where it's quieter," Nick said, and he walked off without looking back. Angus unbuckled himself too and pulled Dummie along behind him.

The stewardess opened a curtain. Behind it, the chairs were further apart from each other. Angus pushed Dummie into a chair next to the aisle, sank into the one next to him, and looked outside. At least Dummie could no longer see the wings from here.

Only then did he look around. There were only two other people in first class. He recognized the man who had been standing behind them in the queue for customs, and next to him was a blond boy wearing a cap.

"Well, if it isn't the burned mummy without a face," the man said in surprise. "Is something the matter?"

The stewardess went over and whispered something in his ear. The man grinned. "Oh, so you're frightened?"

"He thinks the wings should be flapping," Nick said, laughing between his teeth.

"What? They aren't flapping? Oh help, we're goners!" the man cried in mock fear.

Dummie began to scream at once.

"Joke!" The man screwed up his nose, his top lip curled back so much that Angus saw a strip of pink gum and all of a sudden a kind of roar came out of his throat that turned into very loud snorting. "Ha ha ha! Kgrrr! Kgrrr! Kgrrr!"

The man looked very much like a pig to Angus. In any case, it scared Dummie enough to stop him screaming.

"My dad's laughing," the blond boy giggled.

"I'm not. I'm scared witless," muttered Nick, tightening his seatbelt even more.

The man continued to shake for a while and then

cleared his throat. "Do forgive me," he said. "It was just a joke. I'm scared too, you know. People aren't meant to fly, otherwise we'd have wings. But I've got good news for you. I fly all over the world for my work and I've never crashed yet."

"Oh, neither have we," said Nick.

"That's because we've never flown before!" said Angus.

The man had to laugh. "Kgrrr! Kgrrr! Well, my name is Fritz Greystone and this is my son Dimitri."

"I'm Angus," said Angus. "My father's name is Nick and this is Dummie."

"Dummie? He told the customs man he was called Ebbi," Dimitri said cleverly.

Angus could have kicked himself. "Erm yeah. But

since he got burned we've been calling him Dummie,"
he said quickly. "It rhymes with mummy. That's what
he looks like. And because he's from Egypt. Erm, I
mean, his family is there." He blushed. It was obvious
he couldn't lie as well as his dad could. He'd be better
off keeping his mouth shut.

"Oh! Visiting family," Mr Greystone said. "And
Dummie, how long since you last saw your family?"

"More than four thousand…"

"… hours!" said Angus. "And we're not really going to
see them. We're going on holiday."

Luckily the airplane began to turn again then and Nick
began to groan and Dummie began to whine. Angus felt
sick again, but pretended not to be. One of them had to
keep it together, and his father and Dummie were a fat lot
of use.

"You have to do something," Mr Greystone said
friendlily. "Think about something else. Chess for
example. Dimitri, why don't you get out your chessboard
and teach that mummy how to play chess. Angus, you
come and sit next to me if you dare. I'll try not to laugh."

They did this and to Angus' amazement, Mr Greystone was absolutely right. Dummie was distracted just
by them changing places. "I am very ghood at chess," he
boasted. "I will win!"

"Very good," Mr Greystone said contentedly. "And
we'll have something to eat." He pressed the button on
his armrest and a stewardess came over at once. "These
people would like something to eat," he said. "That's
not a problem, is it?" He waved a banknote.

"Of course not," the stewardess smiled. "I'll fetch
something right away."

To Angus' astonishment, a steaming sausage roll was placed on his tray just five minutes later.

"Look Dad, a sausage roll," he giggled.

"And it's already been paid for," Mr Greystone said jovially.

"Well, thank you very much," Angus said, because his father said nothing and was staring at the sausage roll as though it was a roast shoe.

"Oh, my father has enough money," Dimitri said. "He just happens to be the richest banker in the entire country."

"Shh, your mother doesn't like you saying that out loud," Mr Greystone said. "We're just regular people."

Dimitri leaned toward Angus. "That's not true, you know. I usually get taken to school by a bodyguard. My mother is always scared I'm going to get kidnapped. And that I'll have to live in a tiny cupboard and get fed bread and water and have my little finger chopped off and sent to them as proof—'

"That's enough!" Mr Greystone said sternly.

Dimitri stuck out his tongue and began to laugh. His nose went up just as high as his fathers.

"You two laugh in exactly the same way," giggled Angus.

"But at least I snort like a sweet little piglet," hiccupped Dimitri.

"Wait until your voice breaks," chuckled Mr Greystone. "Then you'll sound like a whole sty of old pigs. Kgrrr! Kgrrr!"

Suddenly Angus had a laughing fit. He couldn't do anything about it. He roared with laughter and tears ran down his cheeks.

"What's the matter?" Dimitri asked in surprise.

"I'm five miles up in the sky with two pigs!" Angus shrieked. Then they all fell about laughing, even Nick, although that was probably still just the nerves.

When everyone had stopped laughing and snorting, Mr Greystone told them that he and his son were going to Egypt for a week because they'd shortly be moving there for a year because of his work. "Dimitri's going to spend a couple of days at the international school he'll be going to after the summer holidays. And I'm going to have a look around, at the pyramids and stuff. Hey, I've just had a good idea. I haven't booked a hotel yet, seemed safer that way. If I come to your hotel we can hang out together this week. The boys would enjoy it. And it would be fun for us too, right, Nick?"

To Angus' dismay, Nick thought it a good idea too. But it wasn't! They'd have to watch what they said the whole time. And they wouldn't be able to just do whatever they wanted.

"We already know exactly what where we want to go actually," he said cautiously.

"Not a problem. We'll just go there then too. See, everything settled."

Angus balled his fists. Blasting cackdingle, how could his father be so stupid? He felt a wave of anger wash over him. He'd been looking after his father all morning already because he was worried he'd lose his head. And now they were suddenly going on holiday with Mr Greystone. Well, his father would have to sort it out himself but *he* wasn't going to anymore!

"Why does Dummie talk so strangely?" Dimitri asked.

"Sausage roll," Angus said crossly.

"Sausage roll?"

"It means my father would be better off telling you," Angus said.

Nick did so at once. "Dummie's the son of my mother's cousin. That cousin is half Egyptian because his dad came from Egypt. That's why."

"Aha, so he'll be able to interpret for us," Mr Greystone said excitedly.

"Unfortunately they speak a very strong dialect there," Nick went on, unperturbed. "They live in a tiny village. He understands about as much normal Egyptian as Chinese."

Then he began spontaneously telling them all kinds of things about Dummie. Dimitri shouldn't be surprised if Dummie didn't eat anything at the dinner table because he was on a special diet. They'd brought his food in the suitcase. Dummie called Egypt "his" country all the time because they'd had a school project in which they had to write about a country. "Dummie chose Egypt. That's why he knows so much about it. He still refers to it as "his home" at school." Nick winked at Angus. He was proud of himself too, by the looks of it.

"And which country did you choose?" Dimitri asked Angus.

"Sausage roll," Angus said.

"Spain," said Nick. "Angus knows all about bull-fighting.'

"And Nick knows all about painting," Dummie joined in. "Nick is famous painter. Everyone knows Nick

Ghust. Ghe makes paintings with splats and colours. Ghe sells for ten thousand euro."

Oh no! Angus started feeling hot and moved to the edge of his seat.

He found flying in an airplane with a terrified father and a mummy not just totally exhausting but also really annoying.

The only advantage was that the flight seemed to go very fast. The stewardess even allowed them to stay in first class. Angus thought it was because Mr Greystone had waved another banknote around. From time to time, she came by to ask whether anyone needed any-thing. And one time a lanky man had come into the first class bit, lost and looking for the toilet. Mr Grey-stone had found it terribly funny.

"Kgrrr! Kgrrr! How can you get lost in a plane?!" he'd snorted. The man had winked at Angus. Then he'd quickly got out a camera from his pocket and had taken a picture of Angus and Mr Greystone. Angus burst out laughing, he figured the man had just wanted to come and look at first class. He waved and gave him a thumbs up, and the man quickly took another photo. Nice. He had been caught on camera in first class in an airplane next to the richest banker in the Netherlands. Who else could say that?

After a while Angus' ears began to hurt.

"That means we're going down," Mr Greystone said. "Do your ears hurt too, Dummie?"

"No, I never feel—"

Angus gave Dummie a kick.

"Oh yes. All ears ghurt very much."

"Would you like some chewing gum?"

"No. I never eat. Erm, chewing gum," Dummie said.

"It's because, well, he once choked," Nick started to say. "And then..."

"And then nothing, Dad! He's on a diet!" Angus said. He looked out of the window in irritation. You could see the ground much more clearly now. They were probably flying above the desert because everything was yellow. A while later he saw a lots of square housing blocks and not long after that they were right above the ground. With a small bump, the airplane landed.

"Ladies and gentlemen, we have landed in Cairo," the pilot's voice announced. "Welcome to Egypt. The temperature at this moment is 38 degrees Celsius and there's almost no wind. We hope you've had a pleasant flight and we wish you a pleasant trip."

Dummie pressed his face to the window. "We are there? We are in my ghome?"

"We're on the ground, at least," Nick said in relief. He smiled at Angus. "Now, didn't I do well?"

Angus' jaw dropped. *Do well?* He was never going to fly with his dad again!

They left the airplane, then they bought their visas and Dummie had to go through customs again. But with Mr Greystone things suddenly were a lot easier. He stayed with them, handing out tips here and there and everything went smoothly. Dummie was almost beside himself. "I am ghome!" he shouted with joy. "Outside is my ghome. I will see it now!" He had taken out his camera and was clutching it in his hand. They waited for their suitcases, walked through a hall, went through the revolving doors and then found themselves in the glaring sun.

"Well, this is it then," Nick said.

Dummie looked from left to right and back again. "Is this my country?" he asked in disbelief. "Not possible! Flying donkey went wrong! This is not my ghome!"

"Not so loud. This is a new city in your country," Angus whispered. "It wasn't there back then. We will go to your old town, you know. Please be careful what you say!

Luckily, Mr Greystone was busy arranging transport and Dimitri was taking pictures of his father waving his hands around. Mr Greystone signaled to them and they climbed into a minivan. Angus hurriedly sat down next to Dummie. He pressed his head to the window as though he didn't want to miss a second. They turned into the busy Cairo traffic. Driving around Cairo was exactly like being in a bumper car at the fair. The van shot from left to right across the road, tooting, and a couple of times Angus was thrown forward when the driver slammed on the brakes.

"Has that man even got a driving license?" Nick asked in irritation.

"No," Angus said. He was still angry with his father and it might be true as well because from the looks of things, no one had a driving license. The cars were all over the road, driving unpredictably.

In the end, Nick pulled the curtain in front of his window so he no longer had to look. They jerked and jolted around like this for almost an hour. The entire time, Dummie pressed his face to the window to see whether he could recognize anything of his old country. But the only things they saw were houses and more houses.

Finally they reached the hotel. Nick got out, looking pale. "I feel just like a blancmange," he muttered.

They paid the driver and picked up their keys from the reception. Then they took the lift to the third floor and looked for their room numbers. Mr Greystone and Dimitri had to go left and Nick, Angus and Dummie right. And then they were alone at last.

Angus had never stayed in a hotel. There was a large double bed in the room and a single bed, and apart from that, a small table and chairs, and a cupboard with a television. There was a map of Egypt on the wall and a poster of the famous gold mask belonging to Tutankhamen, which Mr Scribble had told them all about at school.

Dummie lifted up his flap.

"When do we gho to my ghome?" he asked impatiently.

"This is your home," Nick said. "They've built a few houses on it, that's all."

"Yes, I know. But where is my ghome?"

Nick walked over to the map. "We're here now, that's the city," he said. "Look. Here's the Nile. And Sakkara is... erm, here."

"Is that far?"

"Not by the looks of it."

"We gho tomorrow?'

Nick shook his head. "Dummie, Mr Scribble told us the best thing to do. Tomorrow we'll start by visiting the big pyramids at Gizeh. They're still there. And after that we'll go to the museum. They've kept all kinds of important things from the past. And the day after that, we'll go to Sakkara. Alright?"

"MAASHI," Dummie said. "Big pyramids is nice. We can't gho tonight?"

"No. I've been through enough today. And so has Angus. Haven't you, Angus? Angus? What's the matter?"

Finally it dawned on Nick that Angus had barely said a thing since they'd left the airport.

"Are you angry?" he asked in surprise.

"Yes, of course I'm angry," Angus snapped. "I've spent the whole day looking after everyone and I had to arrange everything because you were too scared. I was scared too, you know, but I had to just get on with it. And now you've gone and said Mr Greystone can tag along. How could you do such a thing? Now we'll have to watch what we say the whole time. And all that rubbish you came out with, you just kept adding to it. That's not very clever."

"Actually it was," Nick protested. "I explained why Dummie doesn't eat and why he keeps calling Egypt his home. I had to lie, didn't I? Sausage roll and all that."

"Yes, but not that much. Now we'll have to remember all of those lies. And what are we going to say when we go to Sakkara for five days to look for a grave? He's going to get suspicious then, isn't he? I think you're just scared of being here on your own with us. Am I right or not?"

His father pulled a guilty face. "Well, yes, actually you are. But it's allowed isn't it? Not being tough all the time?" He sighed. "Listen, I've lived in Polderdam all my life and we never went on holiday. And now I've had to go through customs with a living mummy! I had to fly, go in a bumper car and now I'm in some hotel in Egypt. I don't speak the language and I'll have to go looking for a grave. It's not that strange to want to travel with another adult, is it?"

Hmm, no it wasn't, Angus thought. But it wasn't handy either, a scared dad.

"Angus, you helped me a lot today," Nick said. "You were really excellent. You're not staying angry, are you?"

"No," Angus replied automatically. He'd stopped being angry a while ago. He was just worried. "But from now on you have to take care of us again. And not the other way round. And give the sausage roll stories a break."

"I promise," his father said. "By the way, speaking of sausage rolls, I'm feeling rather hungry."

While Nick had a quick shower, Angus went out onto the balcony. Dummie was leaning over the railing, looking down. "Is ghood so ghigh," he said. "City is near Nile. When Nile floods, we won't ghet wet."

"I don't think the Nile floods anymore," Angus said. "Mr Scribble said they've built a dam somewhere."

"What is dam?"

"A kind of wall for the water. It holds the water back when there's too much of it."

"Is that true? Not ghood. The land needs water!"

"Well, I'm sure they've thought of that too. Everything has changed, remember?"

"Yes, I see. New city is ugly," Dummie said. "In my city we have temples. And nice ghouses. And market."

"Oh," said Angus. He looked at Dummie's face. He wished he could read his mind. As far as he could tell, Dummie still hadn't understood that the country as he'd known it no longer existed. Maybe you could only believe a thing like that once you'd seen it. Well,

that would happen soon enough.

Angus had a shower too and after that they sprayed an extra load of toilet freshener on Dummie and went downstairs. Mr Greystone and Dimitri were sitting in the bar drinking coke.

When Nick told them they'd be going to the big pyramids tomorrow and wanted to visit the museum, to Angus' dismay they thougt it was an excellent idea. "Dimitri has to go and meet a couple of people tomorrow afternoon but we can both come with you in the morning," Mr Greystone said cheerfully. Angus had been hoping that they'd rather go on a boat trip along the Nile or something, but it seemed they were never going to get rid of the pair.

He looked the other way and saw the tall man who'd accidentally got lost in the airplane come into the bar. There was a short fat man next to him. The tall man pointed at them and began to wave excitedly. Mr Greystone waved jovially back. "What a coincidence, eh!"

he cried. "Kgrrr! Kgrrr!"

Coincidence? Bad luck more like, thought Angus. More Dutch people. That meant even more watching what they said.

"We want to go to Sakkara too," Angus said. "And to Memphis and all that. But maybe you two would rather do something else this week?"

"No, that sounds great. Wonderful," said Mr Greystone.

Failed. They were never going to get rid of Mr Greystone.

That evening the five of them ate together in the hotel.

"What on earth is this?" Nick asked, pointing at the plate the waiter had brought to him. There was something green and something red on it.

"Very tasty," said Dummie.

"Shame you have to eat out of the suitcase, lad," Mr Greystone said.

Angus looked at his excited face. Mr Greystone considered it totally normal that Dummie wasn't eating. Well, at least his father had succeeded at one thing.

And then that horrible day was finally over.

CHAPTER 3

Dummie's Home

The next morning they got up early. They ate bread rolls, got dressed and put the cards depicting Akhnetut's cartouche in their pockets. Mr Greystone and Dimitri were already waiting for them in the hotel lobby. They were both wearing shorts and their legs were as white as cauliflowers.

Nick, Angus and Dummie were all wearing their straw hats. What's more, Nick had bought an enormous pair of sunglasses and put on his long-sleeved white shirt. "You look ridiculous, Dad," giggled Angus.

"So what? I'm not about to go on a date. I just don't want to get sunstroke, or burned arms," Nick replied.

Mr Greystone had arranged a mini-van for them and not long afterwards, they were back in the busy traffic. Dummie pressed his head to the window in excitement. "Soon I see it! My ghome!" he said, all wound up.

After a while, the van started climbing upwards, along

a wide approach road to three enormous pyramids before parking in front of the biggest one. Angus held his breath. He'd already seen the pyramids in books and on the poster in their classroom. But only now could he see how big they were. He stared at the massive stone hulks in front of him in awe. All those stone blocks, each one was larger than he was! And heavier of course. How had they stacked up those enormous blocks so neatly and then in a perfect pyramid? They certainly hadn't had calculators or big cranes four thousand years ago. It wasn't surprising that Dummie was so proud. Those ancient Egyptians were pure geniuses!

Dummie jumped out of the van with a cry of delight, ran to the pyramid and began to climb it.

"Hey, is that allowed?" Nick cried. "Dummie!"

Dummie turned around, held his arms up in the air and shouted. "MAASHI! Ghere it is! My country! My ghome is still ghere! I am back! Ghooray!" He leapt from one stone to the next like a madman. "Ghooray! DARWISHI UR-ATUM MSMAHI MINKABH ISHAQ EBONI is back!"

"What was that he said?" grinned Mr Greystone.

"Oh, that's Egyptian dialect. He's just happy," Nick said. "Angus, go after him, will you?"

Angus didn't need to be told twice. He ran to the pyramid just like Dummie had done and started climbing. After a couple of blocks, he stopped to catch his breath. How hot it was! And this was just the morning.

Above him Dummie climbed higher and higher. "Yoo-ghoo! Angus! Look!"

Angus looked to his left, there was the city. On the right nothing but stones and sand. "I can see the desert," he shouted.

"Is my ghome!" Dummie rejoiced. "Is nice!"

Angus climbed higher but wasn't able to catch up with Dummie. After a few more blocks, he sat down to

wait for him. Dummie clattered back down again and flopped down beside him. "What do you think?" he asked excitedly.

Angus looked at the hot dry expanse. How could you be so enthusiastic about a lot of stones and sand? He'd rather look at a field of cows. But those pyramids were extraordinary. "Did it used to look the same as now?" he asked, curious to know.

"Desert yes," Dummie said. "But that side was different." He pointed at the city. "Land there was ghreen, sometimes the Nile flooded on it. But not to ghere. And I lived that way. But you can't see it." He pointed in the other direction.

"Was it this hot too?"

"Sun was nice."

"And have you climbed up the pyramid before?"

"No, pyramid slippery. But I ghave been ghere. On donkey. I ghave seen everything. Ghepsetsut take me."

They waved to Nick in his hat down below. "Yoo-hoo! Are you coming?"

Dummie stood up, slipped and before Angus could grab hold of him, he was rolling down like a snowball. He landed on the ground with a nasty sounding thud.

Mr Greystone rushed over to Dummie in shock, but Dummie simply got to his feet, shook his head and started taking pictures. Angus hurried down after him.

"Well, he was lucky. He could have broken his neck," said Mr Greystone.

"Oh, the bandages keep everything intact," Nick said.

"It works like a... erm... an airbag. Since he's had the bandages he's loved falling off things." He winked at Angus as though he'd just come up with something very clever. Well, maybe it was. Dummie was sure to fall off something else and now they already had an explanation.

Once Dummie had got rid of some of his energy, they walked around the pyramids.

Dummie was talking at six to the dozen. "Nile was there before. Pyramid is from ghreat pharaoh, pharaoh called Cheops. Pyramid had golden point to the sky. And city for the builders was there."

"Golly, the things children learn at school these days," Mr Greystone said, impressed.

Dummie and Dimitri took some more photos and walked around the big pyramid. Behind the pyramid there was a small museum and they went inside. In the middle of it, there was a large wooden boat with oars and a small deck which was covered in the middle. As soon as Dummie saw the boat, he grabbed Angus' arm. "What is it doing ghere?" he asked in confusion.

"They found it nearby," Nick read on a cardboard sign. "It was buried next to the pyramid. It looks like a Venetian gondola. Hmm, it's very well-crafted."

"But why is boat ghere?"

"So that everyone can look at it, of course," said Nick.

Angus held Dummie back. "Have you seen that boat before?" he whispered.

"Yes, I know it. Is important."

"What kind of boat is it?"

"Boat is for journey of dead king. Ghoes over Nile to pyramid. I know it. I ghave seen."

"Have you seen this same boat?"

"No, different one."

Before Angus could further reflect on this, his father had pulled him over to a sign. "Look, Angus, there's one of those cartouches!"

Angus looked eagerly at the oval drawing. In the middle there were four hieroglyphics. "Does it say Cheops, Dad?" he asked.

"I don't know. It says sun-chick-snake-chick," Nick said idiotically.

"I know. Says Cheops," said Dummie proudly.

"Can you read that?" asked Dimitri, full of admiration.

"Yes, I can," said Dummie.

"Of course he can't," Angus said quickly. "He just knows a few symbols. From that school project. Come on, show-off." He pushed Dummie ahead of the others. They walked around the boat and were the first ones back outside.

"You need to be more careful about what you say," Angus said urgently. "Or someone will get suspicious. You are just Ebbi, and you can't read hieroglyphics."

He'd only just said this when a voice called out in Dutch, "Look, a mummy!"

Angus spun around. What now?

A little girl ran over to them. "Are you a real one?" she asked inquisitively.

"Of course I am not mummy. I am Ebbi Zanusi," snorted Dummie.

"But he does look like a mummy," Mr Greystone
laughed behind them. "Would you like to have your
picture taken with this real mummy?"

Angus rolled his eyes. The girl was nodding too. To
make matters worse, Dummie was coolly taking off his
T-shirt and trousers so that he was only dressed in his
bandages. He did keep his hat on though, and he stood
next to the girl in front of the pyramid.

Other tourists came rushing over and soon everyone
wanted to have their picture taken with the little mummy. A queue formed. Angus started to feel even hotter
than he had been feeling. He kept a close eye on everyone, but clearly all these people were simply finding it

funny. Two people even gave Dummie some money. Then it was a little boy's turn. He cautiously stood next to Dummie and looked up, somewhat afraid. Dummie took his hand. But before his father could take the picture, the boy had started to scream. "I don't want to! He stinks! And he has golden eyes! Help!"

Angus almost had a heart attack. "That's because of the sun!" he said to the little boy. "Come on, all finished now! We'll be back tomorrow! Bye! Bye! Dummie, put your clothes on!"

For once Dummie listened to him, got dressed and they walked on. Angus shook his head. Keeping an eye on Dummie was going to be a full-time job.

Mr Greystone strode determinedly toward a group of camels. "Right. We're going for a little ride," he said.

"Why?" asked Nick in amazement.

"You can't go to Egypt without a ride on a camel. It's my treat."

"Oh. I'd rather have ice-cream," muttered Nick, pulling a face that suggested another bout of diarrhea might be coming on.

My Greystone began to bargain heatedly with a man with a brown wrinkled face and a turban. Meanwhile, Dummie was studying the large animals with suspicion. "What are they? I've never seen this."

"You've never seen a camel before? Unbelievable," Angus said in disbelief.

"We ghad donkey. This animal is sick. There is bump on back," Dummie said.

"It's supposed to be there. Regular camels have two humps. And if there's just one, it's a dromedary."

"Dummy dairy is odd," Dummie snorted. "I want donkey."

My Greystone paid and turned around. "I've hired all three of them," he said in high spirits. "So, Nick, you'll have one to yourself. Is that alright?"

"I guess so," Nick sighed. He watched mistrustfully as the man with the turban pulled on the heads of the three dromedaries. They animals sank jerkily to their knees. "Well, here we go then," said Nick as he climbed aboard awkwardly. "I must be mad. I never wanted to join the circus... Whaah!"

He struggled to hold on as his dromedary rocked wildly to its feet again.

Angus climbed on behind Dummie, shrieking, "Hold on tight, Dad! We're only going for half an hour."

"Half an hour?!"

Once everyone was seated, the man set off. The three creatures rolled along lazily behind him into the desert. The sun was really strong by now and the stench of the dromedaries was even stronger. They were probably going to catch fleas on top of it, thought Angus. But they looked the part, really Egyptian! "Great, isn't it, Dummie?" he said. "Hey, don't kick."

"Ghave to kick," Dummie said. "Kick makes donkey gho faster."

"Fantastic! They call these animals the ships of the desert!" Mr Greystone called out from the furthest dromedary.

"That doesn't surprise me. All this wobbling around is making me feel seasick!" Nick called back. "Hey, that way! Walk on!" Angus looked back. Nick's dromedary had stopped. Suddenly the creature opened its mouth and to Angus' astonishment something started bulging out. It looked as though a ball was being blown up in its mouth! At the same time there was a deep bubbling sound.

"Whaah!" Nick cried. "My ship's exploding!"

Mr Greystone was beside himself with laughter. "Kgrrr! Kgrr! That's a dulla, a kind of inflatable bit in a camel's mouth. They use it to make a noise," he snorted.

"I suppose you've got the pig's version," cried Nick.

"Whaah! He's doing it again!'

"Don't shout, Dad! He'll bolt!" grinned Angus.

Nick clamped his jaw tight at once. Luckily the dromedary began to walk again and they rolled along some more, before turning around and heading back to the pyramids.

At last they came to a halt. "Hello, sir, me first," Nick gestured, looking pale. The man smiled and pulled the head of Nick's dromedary down. Nick toppled into the sand with a soft plop. "Whumpy dumpman, I'm never doing that again!" he panted, as he scrambled to his feet.

"What does whumpy dumpman mean?" giggled Dimitri.

"Oh, we're not allowed to swear," Angus explained. "That's why my father says whumpy dumpman and I say blasting cackdingle."

Mr Greystone started snorting like a pig again. "Kgrrr! Kgrrr! Then we'll say... Soapy sludgeball. Soapy sludgeball! Soapy sludgeball!"

"Blasting cackdingle!" shouted Angus.

"SIRSAR!" shouted Dummie as he fell from his dromedary with a thud. "Dummy dairy is stupid wuss."

Then they all fell about laughing and couldn't stop.

They beat the sand from their clothes and drank some water.

Dummie had already gone on ahead and suddenly he broke into a run. "There! That one is ghood!" he cried.

"Oh no, what has he seen now?" grumbled Nick.

Angus hurried after him. Dummie was standing next to a man in a long robe who was sitting on the ground next to the pyramid. He had with him a grey donkey. "Akila, Akila," the man said.

"Akila? Same name as my donkey!" Dummie cried in excitement. He stroked the animal's head and ears and patted its neck. Then he got out his camera. "Photo? Maashi?" he asked. The man began to smile, got up and stood next to the donkey. Dummie took the photo and gestured something. The man's smile grew and he gave Akila's reins to Dummie.

"Hey, what are you up to?" Angus asked in concern.

Luckily Nick had already caught up. "No, no, eh... not allowed," he said.

The man said something in English.

"What did he say, Dad?"

"That the donkey isn't going to budge anyway," Nick said in relief. "Well, get up then for a moment, I'll take a picture."

Dummie jumped agilely onto the grey donkey and Nick took his picture. Dummie then sat the wrong way round and Nick took another picture. Then Dummie pulled up his legs and got to his feet. "I stand on donkey!" he called out proudly.

Mr Greystone started snorting again. "Kgrrr! Kgrrr!" The donkey was startled. It pulled its ears back and stared at Mr Greystone, its nostrils trembling. "Hee-haw, hee-haw," it brayed back. Mr Greystone lost it completely now. "Kgrrr! Kgrrr! Kgrrr!" This was too much for the creature. In a single movement, it threw its head back and trotted off.

"Hey!" the man in the robe called out in shock. "Akila! Akila!" But instead of pulling on the reins, Dummie sank down into the saddle and kicked the donkey in its side. "Ghup! Ghup! Nice!" he shouted.

"Not hup hup!" cried Nick. "Angus, go after him!"

Blasting cackdingle, thought Angus. He couldn't keep running after Dummie all the time in this heat. And that donkey was going much too fast! Crossly, he began to run. Dummie steered the animal to a hill, then turned and trotted up another hill. All of a sudden he stopped. Angus caught up with him, panting. "Dummie! You can't keep running off all the time! Dummie?"

Dummie didn't reply. He was sitting stiffly on the donkey with his flap up and his hand around his scarab. He stared tensely into the distance, as though he could see something. Angus looked in the same direction. He couldn't see anything. Or could he? Yes, very far in the distance, he could see the shapes of a number of pyramids. Or were they just rocks? "Is Sakkara over there?" he asked excitedly.

Dummie didn't move, he just sat there on the donkey with his hand on the scarab. "Sadihotep," he muttered. "Sadihotep." Then he kicked against the donkey's belly. Angus quickly grabbed the reins. "Dummie. Dummie! Wake up!"

Finally Dummie turned his head. "What is it?"

"The donkey has to go back! And put your flap down!"

"Maashi. You come on back?" Dummie asked, as though nothing had happened.

Angus shook his head, perplexed. "No. Yes. On the back? Is that possible?"

"Akila is strong, you know," Dummie laughed.

"Oh, alright then." As Angus clumsily climbed on, he tried to memorize the word. Sadihotep. What might that mean?

Dummie urged the donkey on. First he steered it in Nick's direction, who was standing at the pyramid, waving. But then he kicked with his trainers, whipped the reins up and steered to the right. "Maashi! We're going round!" Dummie shouted. They galloped around the big pyramid at breakneck speed. A couple of tourists had to jump out of the way, otherwise the donkey would have run them down blindly. Angus clung on for dear life. "Stop! Stop!" he screamed.

"Donkey do what I want!" Dummie shouted back. "Maashi! Maashi!" To his relief, Angus spotted the man in the robe over Dummie's shoulder. When they'd almost reached him, Akila suddenly stopped in his tracks. Dummie and Angus flew over his head and landed upside down on the ground. Angus scrambled to his feet and sneezed the sand out of his nose. "You're crazy," he said crossly.

"Donkey is crazy!" Dummie protested. He stood up and climbed back on. He whipped the reins impatiently but the donkey wouldn't take another step. "Ghup, Ghup!" Dummie tried. "I'm the boss! Boo! Walk!"

"That animal is even more stubborn than you are," Angus said grumpily.

"Oh really?" Dummie suddenly leaned so far forward that his head hung over the donkey's nose and he lifted up his flap. "Boo!" he cried.

Akila was frightened out of his wits and reared up, causing Dummie to fall off for the second time. The donkey raced off.

"What are you doing? You mustn't show your face!" Angus roared.

"Why? Donkey don't tell anyone," Dummie said.

Angus turned around and saw the man in the robe in the distance, running after the donkey.

The animal must be having a terrible day. First Mr Greystone's snorting, and now Dummie's golden eyes. It suddenly seemed very funny. "That poor donkey!" he hiccupped.

"Yes, poor! My ghome is nice, yes!" Dummie said proudly.

"Yes. And you are terrible!"

They went back to Nick and waited until the man had come back with the donkey.

Mr Greystone gave the man some money and luckily he wasn't annoyed any more after that. But the donkey kept its ears back. It was still a bit cross!

They walked around for a bit and were about to return to the van when Mr Greystone stopped in his tracks. "Hey, it looks like you can go in there," he said. He pointed to a burial mound. A couple of tourists were just coming out of a hole in the wall. They walked over to take a look. Angus looked inside. A small iron ladder lead down into the ground. Next to the entrance, a man gestured that they could go inside if they paid. Angus heart started beating faster. There was a real Egyptian grave down there. And you could just go into it!

"Shall we go, Dad? Are you coming, Dummie? Dummie?"

He looked around. Dummie had stopped.

"Who did that?" he asked with barely contained rage.

"Did what?" Angus asked in surprise.

"Ghrave is open! People gho in!"

"Yes, it's for the tourists. They can see what it looked like in the past. Are you coming? What's the matter?"

"Inside? Not allowed!" Dummie bristled.

Angus thought quickly. Dummie was furious. But why?

Behind them, Mr Greystone had already paid. "Are you coming?" he asked. He disappeared down the hole with Dimitri and Nick.

"I'm sure the tourists don't damage anything," Angus said. "Come with us, then you can see for yourself. Come on now."

Dummie hesitated and then followed Angus, gnashing his teeth. They descended the iron ladder. At the bottom of the ladder there was a narrow passage with lights in the ceiling. The ceiling was so low that even Angus almost had to bend over. "It's like an oven in here," they heard Nick's voice in the distance. "You could easily cook some pizzas. Has anyone ever got stuck here?"

"If my belly can get through, you can too," said Mr Greystone.

"Just as long as your belly doesn't start expanding in the heat," grumbled Nick.

Mr Greystone's snorting echoed through the grave.

Angus cautiously descended further. There was a sharp bend in the passageway and they had to climb down some steep steps. After that there was an empty square-shaped room. Angus stood upright and looked around in disappointment. So this was a burial chamber. The chamber was empty except for a couple of big blocks of stone. There weren't any hieroglyphics on the wall and no treasure on the ground. Against the back wall was an empty stone coffin. In fact, there was nothing exciting to see at all.

"Ghe is empty!" Dummie cried at the same moment. "Where is mummy?"

"Gone. It's been pillaged. Everything stolen," puffed Nick.

Dummie balled his fists. "Who did that?" he snarled.

"It was centuries ago. Grave robbers. Yeah, that's what happens, lad," said Mr Greystone. "Money and valuables always get stolen, nothing new there. But luckily they left the pyramid standing."

"They must be punished!" Dummie hissed.

"Oh, it happened a long time ago," Mr Greystone grinned. "Have you ever heard of the pharaoh's curse? The first people to enter a grave all died in mysterious ways?"

"Is that true?" Angus shuddered.

"Come on, don't scare them," Nick said. "They simply caught the flu."

"Pharaoh flu." Mr Greystone winked at Angus.

"I ghope the curse is real!" Dummie blustered. "I ghope the curse is for people now!"

Mr Greystone looked surprised. "Hey, calm down. Or we'll get it too."

Angus took Dummie's hand. He had to get Dummie out of there before he had a tantrum or started shouting things he'd better not. "We're going. It's too hot in here for me," he said, pulling his friend back up the stairs.

← burial chamber

As soon as they were outside, Dummie began to rant and rave again. "They ghave destroyed my ghome. Ghow is possible? Not allowed. I will ghit thieves!"

"Stop it, Dummie. Those thieves are no longer alive. It all happened a long time ago, a very long time ago. They've been dead for centuries."

"But not allowed! Mummy needs ghouse, for journey! And things, also for journey! Where are things?"

Angus thought quickly. He had to calm Dummie down before anyone got suspicious.

"Listen, a lot of things from the past are in the museum. Where we're going this afternoon. It's... erm... safer. Everyone can see them there. And all the things are looked after really well. There are guards." Pfff, at least that sounded alright.

"Are mummies in the museum too?" Dummie asked angrily.

"Yes, of course. I mean, I think so."

This was the wrong answer because Dummie immediately got even angrier. "You are crazy! Mummies must be in ghrave! SIRSAR! I will take back!'

"You can't," Angus said. "They're guarded. They're simply there now. It's..." Angus shut up. What could he say?

Dummie turned around, walked off and then came back. "I ghave to know! My father's things, in museum too?" he hissed.

"Of course not," said Angus. "Mr Scribble said they never found his grave." Now Angus was suddenly glad they hadn't. "His mummy is still in its sarcophagus and his grave is still full."

"You are sure?"

"Yes," Angus lied. He quickly looked the other way. He wasn't entirely certain. Mr Scribble had told them about graves that had been found and only had the mummy left in them. And he had said that there might be something belonging to Akhnetut in the museum.

An object that had been stolen earlier and had later turned up, something like that. If they found anything like that this afternoon, it would mean that Akhnetut's grave had been robbed. Well, Dummie would probably explode then.

He remembered the word that Dummie had said. "Dummie, what does Sadihotep mean?"

"Sadihotep?" Dummie repeated.

"You whispered 'Sadihotep' on that donkey. Is it something special?"

Nick stuck his bright red face out of the hole. His white shirt was soaking wet and his hat was crumpled. "I feel just like a roast chicken," he panted.

"You look like one too," laughed Mr Greystone, who was climbing out of the hole after him. "A chicken with a straw hat and sunglasses."

Nick wiped his forehead. "Unbelievable. They went to so much effort for a grave in those days. What a pity it's completely empty."

"Shhh!" Angus hissed. He elbowed his father in warning and pointed at Dummie.

Nick didn't understand, but luckily he did keep his mouth shut. He looked up. The sun was almost directly above their heads.

"Shall we go back to the hotel?" he asked. "At least they have air-conditioning there."

"No. We gho to museum," Dummie said abruptly.

"Alright. Let's go and see if we can find anything of your dad's in there," Nick said.

Dummie said nothing, but Angus saw him ball his fists again. He had to tell his father not to say stuff like that.

Unfortunately he didn't get the chance, because in the van, Nick immediately sat down next to Mr Greystone. And just when they were about to drive off, two other men ran over to the van. Angus recognized the two Dutch men from the hotel. "Are you going to the hotel? Can we get a lift with you?" they panted.

So they drove into Cairo with a full van. The men wanted to get out a little bit before the hotel. And not long after that, they dropped off Mr Greystone and Dimitri. And then the three of them went to the museum.

Angus still hadn't been able to warn his father. The closer they got to the museum the more nervous he felt. Just as long as they didn't find anything belonging to Akhnetut, he thought.

"I hope we find something belonging to your dad," Nick said at the same moment. And then Angus gave him another shove. "Stop pushing me. That's what we came for, isn't it?"

Dummie said nothing and looked out of the window.

Angus leaned back. Sadihotep, he said to himself. I mustn't forget that word.

sadihotep

The museum was a big pink building in the city centre.
Nick bought three tickets, they went through an enormous door and then found themselves in a massive
hall. Angus' mouth fell open. The hall was filled with
statues, statues and more statues. They were enormous,
some of them six times as big as he was. There were
hundreds of people looking at the statues and there
were groups with guides all shouting at the same time.
It was horribly busy.

"Wait here a sec," said Nick. He went away and came
back with a brochure containing a map of the museum.
"More than a hundred thousand objects," he read out
loud. "Well, that will keep us busy. Shall we start with
the statues then?"

This was safe enough, Angus thought. The statues
came from temples and not graves. Hopefully Dummie
wouldn't be angry if they found a statue of Akhnetut.

"That cartouche, Dad, that signature. That's what we

have to look for." They got out their cards with Akhnetut's cartouche and began to walk. Some of the statues had a cartouche on their pedestal, and others on their clothes or a bracelet. But some didn't have a cartouche at all.

"Dummie, did your dad have a statue like this?" Angus asked.

"I don't know," said Dummie hesitantly. "I think so. Statues of all pharaohs were in temple. That one too. And that one." Angus glanced at the statues Dummie was pointing at, but their cartouches didn't look anything like Akhnetut's. It wasn't surprising that Dummie was wrong, they all looked the same.

Nick paused to listen to a guide speaking English. "And?" Angus asked.

"I couldn't understand all of it," said Nick. "But the ones with the weird goatees are pharaohs. And if they have two crowns they ruled over North and South Egypt. And they all look alike because they wanted to be remembered after their deaths as beautiful young people. Something like that."

"That won't help us much," Angus said.

"No," Nick said. "But it is interesting."

They carried on and passed more statues without a cartouche, all kinds of objects in glass cases and large stone sarcophagi. After half an hour, Angus started to feel dejected. They could spend a whole week in here and still they wouldn't have seen everything.

Dummie walked from one statue to the next and then to a display case. Apparently he'd forgotten how angry he was. "Is nice! Is all from my ghome!" he said proudly.

After a while, they'd seen all of the rooms representing the oldest dynasties. They hadn't found Akhnetut's cartouche anywhere. They spent the next half hour roaming the rest of the ground floor. But it was simply too much. Everything Angus saw, he forgot again immediately. In the end, all he looked at were the cartouches. He'd be able to spot Akhnetut's cartouche in his sleep by now, but it was nowhere to be found. He walked slower and slower, he was getting hotter and hotter and he started to see double. By the end he no longer knew whether he'd already looked at a statue or not.

"I'm seeing so much I'm no longer seeing anything," he panted. "Shall we go upstairs? Maybe it won't be as crowded there."

Nick leafed through the brochure. "I don't think so. All the treasures of Tutankhamen are upstairs," he said.

"Tutankhamen?" Angus woke up now. "Is that mask there too?"

"I think so," said Nick.

"Then I want to go! Come on."

Filled with new energy, they mounted the stairs. Unfortunately Nick was right. It was even more crowded in the Tutankhamen rooms. The chatter was deafening and everyone was secretly taking pictures. Angus really wanted to see the famous mask, but it was so famous everyone else wanted to look at it too! He had to wait ten minutes before it was his turn. The mask was in a glass case and it shone as though it had just been polished. Angus stared in awe at its shining eyes, the blue goatee and the crooked snake on top of the head. What a waste to have buried a thing like that!

It was a long time before he turned around and walked away. Tutankhamen's sarcophagus was in the same room as the mask. Or more accurately: his sarcophagi. Tutankhamen had been buried in four enormous golden coffins and three golden sarcophagi. "Well, he wasn't likely to escape," Nick laughed. "And look at this! What a lot of treasure!" He pulled Angus along with him. Angus could hardly believe his eyes. Seven coffins was already crazy. But there were another ten rooms containing all of the treasures from the grave. Thrones, funeral biers, a boat, countless objects, jewelry, chairs and little dolls. "All of that in one grave?" he asked in disbelief.

"They piled it all up, I believe," Nick said drily. "Angus, there's a fortune in gold here! What a waste to have buried it. What's the point of it when you're already dead?"

"It's for the journey or something. That's what Dummie said," Angus replied. Now it struck him why Dummie had been so upset at the pyramids. If those pharaohs from the past had been given that much stuff so that they could travel on after their death, it must have been really important.

He looked around. Dummie was sitting on a bench with his hand around his scarab, his head at a slant. Angus walked over to him. "See that everything is being properly looked after," he whispered. "It's all behind glass. There are guards everywhere. If you left that kind of gold just lying around, it would definitely be stolen. It's a lot, isn't it?"

Dummie nodded. "I know. I went to funeral. I ghave seen even more stuff than this."

Angus leaned in closer. "Dummie, think carefully. What kind of stuff? What can you remember? Which procession were you in? Was it in your dream? Who was being buried? Was it a pharaoh?"

Dummie shook his head. "I know, and then not," he said. "I want to look at more."

So they carried on, combing room after room. They saw dozens of sarcophagi, and heaps of jewels, items of clothing and shoes. Hundreds of statues, mummies and drawings on papyrus paper. Every time Dummie paused a display case, Angus kept a careful eye on him. Some of the stuff must have come from graves, but luckily Dummie didn't find anything of his father's.

When they entered a new room, Angus stopped in his tracks. There were all kinds of mummified animals on display. "Did they have to go on a journey too?" he asked in amazement. "Look at this! A bird! A monkey! And a crocodile mummy! Why did they do this?"

Nick looked up animal mummies in his booklet. "Some animals were holy animals in temples, or used as sacrifices," he read aloud. "And some animals were put in the graves as food, or as pets."

"Did they keep crocodiles as pets?!"

"Sure, they love to sit on your lap," Nick joked. "No, of course not. That crocodile must have been a Nile god.

The Nile was very important to them."

Angus went from one case to the next. He saw a snake. A whole donkey! This was the best room in the museum!

After a while, Nick tapped him on the shoulder. "Angus, I'd like to go back to the hotel soon," he said. "I can't look at any more stuff, it's going in one eye and out the other. And I don't think there's even a toenail belonging to Akhnetut in the place."

"Just as well," Angus said. "Do you know why Dummie got so angry at the pyramids? He said..."

"Where is Dummie in fact?" Nick interrupted.

Angus looked around in shock. "Dummie? Dummie!"

They ran through the rooms. Angus was getting more and more worried. Had Dummie found something? Or had he just walked off? What if they never found him! Suddenly he spotted the straw hat. Dummie was standing with his nose pressed to a glass case. "Dummie!" Angus called out.

"That one! I know! Come ghere!" Dummie cried excitedly. He pointed at a large golden sceptre behind the glass.

"Was it your dad's?" Angus asked in shock.

"No! Not Akhnetut. I know for sure."

Angus sighed in relief. "But you do recognize it? Whose was it then?"

"Father of my father. I know for sure!"

"What?" Angus quickly looked around. "Not so loud! Your father's father? Who was that? You've never talked about him."

"Because I only remember now. Now I see. From funeral. From my dream!"

Angus' mind raced. Here was something that had belonged to Akhnetut's father, Dummie's grandfather. Dummie must have been to his grandfather's funeral. Oh, how stupid! Yes, of course. Why hadn't he thought of that before? A funeral procession that went to a pyramid... If Dummie had seen a pharaoh's burial it could only have been his grandfather's! "Dad, that dream! Dummie was at his grandad's funeral, it must be! And after that, Akhnetut became pharaoh, of course. And after that Dummie died, and just after that so did Akhnetut! That's how it went! Nothing else fits!"

Nick looked at Angus, staggered. By the looks of it he was also kicking himself for not thinking of this. "Mr Scribble didn't think of it either," he said sheepishly.

"Sadihotep, Sadihotep," said Dummie.

"Yes, dentist's drill, mandarin peel," Nick replied.

"Don't be silly, Dad." Angus grabbed Dummie's arm, "Sadihotep? What does that mean? That's the word you said this morning at the pyramids when you were riding the donkey. What does Sadihotep mean?"

"It is name of old king, of course.'

Angus was perplexed. "Was that your grandad's name? Was the father of your father called Sadihotep? And that was his sceptre? Really? Dad! This is amaz... Dad, what's the matter?"

Angus was surprised to see his father hurriedly leafing through his booklet. "I think I saw that Sadi-thingy somewhere in here," he said excitedly. "Hang on. Yes, here. Here it is! "In room 52, you'll find the mummies of the kings of the Old Kingdom, the Middle Kingdom and the New Kingdom." And under that it says... Look, read this!"

Angus looked in disbelief at the third name in the list. "Sadihotep!" he whispered.

Nick gave Dummie a triumphant look. "Whumpy dumpman, Dummie, your grandad in is the museum!"

Angus' heart began to beat wildly. Dummie's grandad here in the museum? That was amazing! Or no! It might actually be awful!

He laid his hand on Dummie's shoulder and looked at him pleadingly. "Dummie, please don't get mad. Your grandad is here. No one can do anything about it. Shall we go and take a look?"

To his relief, Dummie nodded. "Of course I want to look. Where is room?"

"Near the stairs, at the side. I think you have to pay extra for it, though," said Nick.

"So what," cried Angus. "Let's go!"

Angus, Dummie and Nick practically ran to the other side of the museum. Nick bought three tickets and a few seconds later they were walking down the corridor to the room with the mummies of the kings. Angus held Dummie's hand tightly. He was about to see his grandad's mummy! As long as he didn't start shouting crazy things.

"Alright, here we go," Nick said.

They entered the hall. It was much quieter here. There were much fewer people and everyone was walking slowly and whispering. There were large glass cases along the walls and in the middle of the room. Angus approached the nearest case, bent over and stared right into the face of a dried up mummy. He had the fright of his life. He stepped back, horrified. Its face was uncovered. The whole mummy was practically naked! It wasn't even in a sarcophagus or anything but just lying on its bare back on the glass. Luckily there was a cloth over the body, but its skinny arms and feet were sticking out. Its skin was black with brown and grey patches and its feet were almost entirely black. Angus shuddered. Here he was, looking at a skeleton with a torn brown layer of skin around it. It was just horrible!

He quickly glanced around the room. The other people were walking around the glass coffins, having a good look at everything. Some of them stood staring open-mouthed right into the scary faces of these naked horrors.

Angus looked back and thought about what Dummie looked like under his bandages. Exactly the same in fact. But Dummie had been living with them for months and they'd got used to him by now. Or rather, he did sometimes find Dummie horrifying but it was an endearing kind of horrifying.

There was a white card at the foot of each mummy and it had the name and a bit of text. Angus read the name without looking at the fraying toes. Phew. This wasn't Sadihotep.

He walked on to the next coffin and got a new shock. This mummy had been unwrapped just the same and had a mop of hair like a scarecrow's. But it wasn't Sadihotep. Neither was the next one. The one after that still had lots of strips of linen around it, luckily, but it wasn't Sadihotep either.

Nick crossed the room to the other side. He was finding it just as horrible because his expression was like he'd stepped in ten dog poos at the same time.

"Ghere!" Dummie called out suddenly.

Angus and Nick hurried to the case at the furthest corner of the room. Angus closed his eyes, took a deep breath and then opened them again. "Blasting cackdingle," he whispered. Sadihotep was one of the most horrifying mummies in the room, that much was certain. Just like the other kings, he lay on his back. His chin was raised and his mouth was half open, which made it look like he was grinning. Here and there, strands of whitish yellow hair stuck up on top of his head. He still had half of a black nose, the other half had gone. His neck was scarily thin and his arms were still wrapped in bandages, but even they were nothing but bone, it seemed. One arm stuck up at a funny angle, as though he wanted to wave.

Angus bit his lips. He wanted to say something but what? *What a nice grandad? Seems like a nice man*

"What does it say, Dad?" he asked nervously.

Nick quietly translated the English words on the card at Sadihotep's feet. It was just a short text. Sadihotep was a king from the sixth dynasty of the Old Kingdom. He'd been found last century in a granite sarcophagus in a small pyramid in Sakkara. That was it.

Dummie stood motionlessly beside the case and clutched his scarab in his hand. "Sadihotep," he whispered.

Nick moved behind him, gently laid his hands on Dummie's shoulders and rubbed. They stood like this for a while, just looking.

"Are you sure this is your grandad?" Angus whispered all of a sudden. Now it seemed impossible to him. He could see the difference between one mummy and the next. Some were a bit scarier. But none of them looked like living beings.

"I am sure," Dummie whispered. "Finger is ghone. From ghunting accident."

Blasting cackdingle! Dummie was right. On his left hand Sadihotep only had four fingers, the middle one was missing. This couldn't be a coincidence! This really was Dummie's grandad! Or in any case what was left of him.

Dummie pressed his face to the glass and balled his fists. Angus started to feel more and more uncomfortable. Was Dummie about to explode with rage? Or was he simply sad? Maybe he was praying or something. To Dummie, Sadihotep wasn't a horror at all. It was his grandfather. Had Sadihotep taught him how to ride a donkey? Or played with him? Was he thinking about that now? It was hardly imaginable.

Nick let go of Dummie and gently pulled Angus away until they were a few feet from Sadihotep. "Leave him for a moment," he said quietly.

"He looks weird, doesn't he?" Angus whispered.

"Weird? Terrifying more like."

"Dad! Don't say that. It's Dummie's grandad!"

"I am saying that. They're all terrifying. All these naked skeletons in this aquarium. It's like a house of horrors. I'm glad they're behind glass."

"I wouldn't touch them, you know," Angus said.

"No, I mean so they can't touch us. Just imagine..."

"Dad! Don't be silly. That's the kind of thing kids say. It's totally impossible."

"Really? What about Dummie then?"

Angus suddenly imagined the glass cases opening and mummies stepping out. Whaah! It was even more horrible. This was the stupidest room in the museum! It was normal to put art or old objects in a museum. But dead people, that wasn't normal, was it? And they'd even paid to see this!

"Maybe Akhnetut is here too," Nick whispered.

"He wasn't on that list, was he? They never found his grave."

"No, but you never know. Let's check just to be sure."

They looked into a new coffin and Angus almost screamed. Before him lay a mummy with a wide open mouth, and Angus was staring straight into the hole where his throat had once been.

"Whumpy dumpman, this one wins the beauty contest," muttered Nick. "I say, put him straight back under the ground, in ten golden coffins at the same time, with some very good locks on them."

Angus almost laughed nervously. Fortunately, he was in total agreement with his father again.

Angus and Nick checked all the other glass cases and their descriptions as fast as they could while staying discreet. Akhnetut's mummy wasn't among them. That was lucky, it would have been a real disaster.

Dummie was still staring at his grandad. Finally he turned around and came back to them. "I ghave seen," he said. "I want to gho to pyramid."

Nick wrapped his arms around him. "Then we'll go to your grandad's pyramid tomorrow," he said. "And now, I think we should leave."

At the door, Dummie turned back and gazed into

the corner again. He heaved a sigh and then they were back in the museum's noisy hall.

"And now?" Angus asked softly.

"I want to go back to sceptre," said Dummie.

When they were in front of it, he tugged at Nick's sleeve. "I want sceptre," he said. "Is mine."

"Yes. Erm, no, that's impossible," Nick said uneasily.

"You must buy. With my money."

"It's not for sale."

"But ghe is mine! We will steal!"

"No!"

Dummie balled his fists. "Then I want to look more."

They reluctantly roamed around the museum for another thirty minutes. But there was nothing else in the entire museum that Dummie recognized. Nothing belonging to Sadihotep and, luckily, nothing belonging to Akhnetut.

Finally they were back outside. It was still hot. They looked for an empty taxi and jolted back to the hotel.

Dummie stared ahead. "Sadihotep should be in pyramid," he said. "You will fix it?"

"Who, me?" Nick asked. "It's up to the Egyptian government. Or someone else. But not me."

"But ghe belongs in pyramid," said Dummie. He was quiet for a moment. "How many pharaohs ghave there been?"

"Erm, maybe a hundred," Nick said.

"Not so many in museum. Where are other mummies?"

"Still buried somewhere," Nick said. "Or in other museums. I think they even shipped some of the mummies abroad. As a present, because people from other countries helped to dig them up."

"Mummie as present?!" Dummie asked in dismay.

Angus gave his father a shove. He really shouldn't have said that.

"You were in a museum too, in Holland," he said quickly. "But all those other museums take really good care of them too. Just like here. Tell us about your grandad. Was he nice?"

"Of course ghe was. Ghe ghad nice palace. And was strict with enemy. But not with me. Ghe ghave me donkey. And now ghe is there." Dummie lifted up his flap and looked at Angus. His golden eyes glowed. "Sadihotep is in museum," he said. "Ghe cannot gho back in ghrave. Nothing can gho in ghrave. I ghet it. But I am ghoing to find my father's ghrave. My father must be in ghrave. Must!" he said.

Angus took Dummie's hand and squeezed. "And he is," he said, hoping it was true.

When they got back to the hotel, Mr Greystone was thankfully nowhere to be seen.

"I've got an idea," Nick said. He went over to the

desk, asked something in English and handed over some money. "I did it! We can use one of the hotel's computers," he said. "Come on, we can use the internet for half an hour."

At the back of the reception were a couple of tables with computers on them.

Nick sat down and typed in "Sadihotep". A few seconds later they were looking at a photo of Dummie's grandfather in the museum. "Unbelievable. If only we'd known his name earlier," Nick muttered. "It says he's from the sixth dynasty and he's got a pyramid in Sakkara. Well, we knew that already. But not much besides. I don't think they know a lot about that period. Oh, it does mention the finger. Got lost in a fight."

"No, ghunting," Dummie corrected him.

"Fine, hunting is like fighting. Let's have a look, he was buried in Sakkara... Sakkara... Sadihotep's grave... This must be it," Nick said. "Look, here's a map of the burial ground. So those blocks must be pyramids, and... Got it. Dummie, brace yourself... this is your grandad's pyramid." He clicked triumphantly on a block. A large mound of stones appeared.

"What?" Dummie looked at the messy pile in disbelief. "Not possible. Not ghood. Pryamid is slippery. And where is temple? And nice road to Nile? And wall? This is not ghood."

Nick clicked a few more times but the same mound of stones came into view. He scratched his chin. "It really is it, though," he said. He clicked some more. "Look, this is a drawing of what it must have looked like. With a temple and a wall around it, and a long road to the Nile. They found that out, erm, later. Is this right?"

"Yes! That is! I know! From dream! Where is it?"

Nick showed him the photo of the stones again. "It's here," he said gently. "This is all that's left."

"All? Nothing more? Sɪʀsᴀʀ!" Dummie stamped his foot in disappointment.

Angus was just as disappointed. All there was left of what was on the drawing was a big pile of stones. This didn't bode well for Akhnetut's grave. If this was all there was left of a big pyramid, there wouldn't be much left of a simple tomb. How would they ever find it?

"What's written next to it?" he asked.

Sadihotep's grave was at the edge of a large burial ground. They only discovered the entrance last century. There was a narrow corridor down to a gallery, and behind it a temple and a burial chamber. They were both empty when they were found, only the mummy's sarcophagus was left. The mummy was examined and taken to the museum.

"But Dad, why is it such a, erm— mess? The pyramids at Gizeh are much older and in better condition."

"Because—" Nick continued to search. "Here. The Gizeh pyramids were made from large fitted blocks. On the inside too. But the Sakkara pyramids were made of loose stones on the inside. They did use smooth blocks for the outside, but later they were used for other buildings. Like a kind of quarry." He looked up. "Well that's nice. They simply stole the outside bits."

"It doesn't say anything about the sceptre?"

"No. It must just be chance that it's in the museum."

Dummie got up and stood silently looking at the screen.

"So we can go to your grandad's pyramid," Angus said. At least that was something. Even if they didn't find Akhnetut's grave, at least Dummie would have been to his grandad's. But Dummie wasn't happy at all. "That is not pyramid! That is pile of stones without mummy! And things are ghone! I gho to room!"

He spun around and walked toward the lifts.

Angus looked at Dummie's sagging shoulders and felt his stomach sink. Blasting cackdingle. It was all going wrong. They simply hadn't thought this through properly. And neither had Mr Scribble. What had he said? First show him something that still exists. The big pyramids and the museum. Well, they'd done that. But Dummie had got angry at the pyramids, because you were allowed inside, and he'd found his grandad in the museum who really should have been in his grave. Let him say goodbye in Sakkara, Mr Scribble had said. They'd do that tomorrow, in an empty grave in a mound of collapsed stones. Everything was gone, broken, or in the wrong place.

"It's all so complicated, Dad, isn't it?" he sighed. "I'm not really enjoying it. Dummie can't understand what all that stuff from the graves is doing in a museum. We think it's pretty, but Dummie thinks it's awful."

"We think differently from the ancient Egyptians," said Nick. "But Dummie still thinks the same way. Because he *is* an ancient Egyptian."

"His home country simply doesn't exist anymore, does it?" said Angus.

Nick shook his head. "Dummie is back in Egypt. But in fact he's even further from home than ever. I don't think we should even look for his father's grave. What if we find it and Akhnetut ends up in a fish tank too. Dummie would explode." He scratched his chin. "If you think about it, it's totally bonkers. If we started messing around with a Dutch grave, we'd be fined. But here they simply rob the joint."

"Maybe because there aren't any relatives left to be upset by it?" said Angus.

"Well, then they'd be wrong," Nick said. "Here's the room key. Hurry after him. And I'll carry on searching."

Angus took the lift upstairs. Dummie was sitting on the floor in front of their room. Angus opened the door and Dummie went straight out onto the balcony. Angus sat down next to him on the little bench. "Hey Dummie, are you still angry?"

"Yes. No. I am all."

There was silence. "It's... Shall we..." Angus stopped. What could he say? "We have found your grandad's grave in any case," he said simply. "That's good, isn't it?"

"Not ghood. Sadihotep must gho in ghrave with stuff for journey."

That journey again, thought Angus. "What kind of journey then?"

"Journey after death. When you are dead, you gho on journey. Everyone knows that, no?"

Angus shook his head not understanding. Dummie looked at him as though he was incredibly stupid. Then he began to explain. "When you are dead, you gho on journey to Osiris. You see many more ghods there, bad and ghood. There is also Nut. Ghoddess who eats the sun every day," he said.

"Eats the sun?" Angus repeated sheepishly.

"You are so stupid! Where do you think sun ghoes at night?"

"To the other side of the world, of course," said Angus.

"There is just one side!" Dummie snorted. "Sun is in belly of Nut!"

Angus shook his head in bewilderment. Dummie even believed the world was flat! Dummie continued to explain: you could only go to Osiris if your heart was lighter than a feather, and it was weighed by another god. There was a dangerous journey across a river, in a boat. It was a long journey, but afterwards you'd stay in gheaven with Osiris forever. "That is why body and gheart must stay ghood," said Dummie. "That is why we make mummy. Mummy is ghard work. First everything out of belly, stomach too, but gheart must stay. And brains out of ghead too, through ghole in nose. Or ghole in ghead, also possible. But everything must gho in ghrave. In jar. Four jars. And when belly and ghead are empty, they put white stuff over belly and ghead. The stuff makes it dry. Arms and legs ghet very thin. Then some oil, and then bandages. Lots and lots. Takes very long time."

Angus listened on the edge of his seat. At last Dummie stopped.

"How do you know all that?" Angus asked.

"Because I ghave seen, of course. With Sadihotep."

"What? You saw your grandad being made into a mummy?" Blasting cackdingle, it hardly bore thinking about.

"I did not want to see," said Dummie. "But Ghepsetsut made me. Ghe say it ghood if I know everything." He got up and stared into space. "I find it scary, but is ghood. But was for nothing. Sadihotep now on journey without ghrave and stuff."

Angus felt awful about it. He'd never seen it this way. All those people in the museum just thought the mummies were creepy and interesting. But that whole mummy thing was really important. He looked at Dummie's back. He had to cheer up his friend.

"Dummie, how long does that journey take?"

"Why?"

"Well, I mean, your grandad has been dead for a long time, he must have got to Osiris by now, right? And then he won't need his stuff anymore."

Dummie turned around. "Stuff is for there too! You understand nothing! If you are dead and gho on journey, you do not want to be present for museum! Do you?"

"Erm, no. Or in actual fact..." Angus considered it seriously. To be honest, he wouldn't really care. Maybe in the first few years. But not after four thousand years. "I don't even know whether I'll go on a journey after my death," he said.

"No journey? Don't be stupid! Everyone ghoes on journey!"

"Maybe not," Angus said cautiously. "That thing about the journey, that's what people used to think. But now they think something else. Some people think you go to heaven, and others think that you come back again. And some think that you're simply dead."

"Can't. People is stupid."

"Not true. It's just a different time. People simply think something different now."

"And who is right?" asked Dummie.

Angus said nothing. Who could answer this? Not even Mr Scribble knew the answer. Nobody knew. But they thought different things all over the world, he knew that. And your body was no use to you when you were dead, he was sure about that. And neither were those belongings. If you were dead, you were simply buried in a coffin. And after a while there was nothing left of you, except a few bones. "We bury people in the ground," he explained. "Without all that mummy stuff. And after a while the worms have eaten you up."

"Eaten up? But you are not bread?" Dummie said indignantly.

Angus didn't much like the sound of it either really. Maybe it was better to be in a pyramid surrounded by golden objects and mummified crocodiles.

They sat in silence for a bit.

"Where's your mum?" Dummie asked suddenly.

Angus started. They'd never talked about his mum. His mother had died when he was only six months old. "I never knew her," he said. "I've always been with my dad. Nick is my mum and my dad. There's no other way it can be and that's fine."

"But where is she?" Dummie insisted.

"You know. In heaven, of course," said Angus.

"Do you gho to ghrave?"

"No. There is no grave. She drowned at sea. She was never found." Angus hesitated. "But she is in heaven, I'm sure of that."

"Is she with Osiris?"

"Osiris?" Angus had no idea. He'd only heard of Osiris for the first time today. "I don't think so."

"But Osiris is in gheaven."

"Well, then she is. Or... maybe in a different heaven. Maybe your heaven was full. Yes, that would be possible, wouldn't it?"

Dummie had to think about this. And Angus too. It did seem quite logical. All those dead people from the whole world, they'd never fit in just one heaven. "Maybe you can choose," he said.

"Then I choose Osiris," Dummie said at once. "My dad is there too. With things from ghrave. Must be."

Angus thought about what his father had said in the lobby. "You know, Dummie, maybe it would be better if we didn't find your dad's grave. Then he would be able to travel on undisturbed. Let's not look. And then tomorrow we can go to your grandad's pyramid and you can say goodbye and it will be fine. Alright?"

"No. I will find. And I won't tell people," Dummie insisted stubbornly.

"But Mr Scribble said..." Angus hesitated.

"Well, what did he say?" Dummie asked.

"He said we'll never find it," Angus said reluctantly.

"What does ghe know? Is my ghome!" Dummie said angrily. "I gho to sleep. I want to see dream."

He went back into the room, climbed into bed and soon he was indeed asleep.

Angus sat down on his own bed. He felt like he'd just swallowed a brick. Dead bodies, death, he really didn't want to think about those things. He didn't want to think about what it would be like when he was gone, well, he'd find out then. Maybe he would go on a journey. But it was nothing to worry about now, was it? And then Dummie had suddenly brought up his mother...

The door opened and Nick came in.

"Shhh, Dummie's asleep," Angus quickly said, pulling his father onto the balcony. It was still hot. "Did you find out anything else?"

"No," said Nick. "I had another look at Sakkara. It's a very large burial ground, full of graves. Not just belonging to pharaohs, but also to important people who wanted to be buried near them. And not just that. Next to each pyramid was a temple and there were roads to the Nile, and more temples on those. But it's all been stolen or has crumbled away. The temples are gone and so are the roads. Mr Scribble was completely right. If you wait long enough, everything disappears. Oh, and I looked up dromedaries. They didn't have them yet in Dummie's time. They only had oxen and donkeys."

Angus sighed. It was much worse than he thought. Even the animals were different.

"How is Dummie?" Nick asked.

"He's angry. Mainly about the graves being open, and everything taken out. Dummie can't stand the idea." Angus told his father all the things Dummie had explained, the journey after death to Osiris and the goddess Nut who ate the sun every day in the west. And then the mummies. When he was explaining the pots containing the innards, his father shuddered. "What a nasty habit," he shuddered.

"Us being eaten by worms is nasty too, you know," said Angus.

"Yeah," said Nick. "But you don't feel it."

"Neither do the mummies."

Angus paused. "Dad, there's something else," he said then.

"What?"

"Are there... is there more than one heaven?"

"More than one heaven? Why do you ask?"

"Dummie asked where Mum is," Angus said. "My Mum. Is she with Osiris too? Or someone else?"

Nick held his breath for a moment. Then he let out a deep sigh. He got up, laid his strong hands on Angus' shoulders and stared into the distance. "I don't know, son," he said gently.

"But you must have thought about it sometimes?"

Nick shook his head. "You can think about those kinds of things endlessly," he said. "But you can never know anything for sure."

"Dummie is sure about Osiris."

"Yes, and other people are sure about other gods. Some people are so sure they start arguments about it. But there's one thing I am certain about."

"What's that then?" Angus asked.

"Your Mum is in the nicest heaven there is. Just as true as I'm standing here," Nick said. "And the two of us are here. And we're doing very well together."

"Very ghood," Angus said automatically. He closed his eyes and leaned against his father. His dad could be quite awkward sometimes but he always knew everything about the most important matters.

Dummie slept on and on. Nick and Angus went downstairs and quickly ate something in the hotel restaurant. Mr Greystone and Dimitri had got back from Dimitri's school. Dimitri couldn't stop talking about the lovely building and the children who spoke English. He could speak it a bit himself too.

Nick said that they'd be going to Sakkara the next day, to Sadihotep's pyramid because they'd seen his mummy in the museum and thought it was one of the best mummified kings. "Dummie wants to write about it for his project," Nick lied.

"Were there real mummies in the museum?" Dimitri asked excitedly. "What did they look like? Were they frightening?"

Angus and Nick looked at each other. "Well, no, they still looked quite good," Nick lied again.

"And what could be frightening about a mummy?" Angus said. "They used to be nice people too, once."

They hurriedly finished their food, said goodnight and went back upstairs.

That evening they stayed in their room. Dummie slept on and on and finally Nick and Angus went to bed too.

As Nick began to snore, Angus thought about Akhnetut's grave. To be honest, he just wanted to go home now. All of a sudden, he heard a sound next to him. He lifted up the covers and looked at his friend. Dummie was muttering something incomprehensible and clutching his scarab in his hand. He must be dreaming again.

Angus rolled over and tried not to think about anything at all.

Chapter 5
sakkara

It is hot in the burial chamber. Oil lamps cast
shadowy light on the walls.

Darwishi is kneeling on the floor, dipping
his brush into the paint. He carefully paints a
bird. And another one, and another one. Three
large white ibises with long black necks and
legs, long curving beaks and black wing-tips.
He takes a step back and proudly inspects his
picture. This is Kadihotep's pyramid. His grandad
is going to live here after his death and
Darwishi is allowed to do a drawing in amongst
all the drawings by the most important artists
in the country. He likes ibises, they are
pretty. They come when the Nile floods and

LEAVE AGAIN WHEN THE LAND HAS DRIED OUT.

THERE ARE FOOTSTEPS AND HEPSETSUT PUTS A HAND ON HIS SHOULDER.

"DO YOU LIKE THEM?" DARWISHI ASKS.

"I LOVE THEM," SAYS HEPSETSUT. "DID YOU KNOW THESE BIRDS BELONG TO THE GOD THOTH? HE IS THE GOD OF THE MOON, WISDOM AND WRITING."

"OH," SAYS DARWISHI. THERE ARE SO MANY GODS THAT HE CAN'T REMEMBER THEM ALL.

"ON HIS JOURNEY THROUGH THE UNDERWORLD SADIHOTEP WILL MEET THOTH WHEN HIS HEART IS WEIGHED. AND AFTER THAT THOTH WILL TAKE YOUR GRANDFATHER TO OSIRIS," SAYS HEPSETSUT.

"I DON'T REALLY CARE ABOUT THAT," DARWISHI SAYS. "I JUST THINK THEY ARE PRETTY."

HIS TONGUE STICKING OUT, HE PAINTS THE LAST BIRD WHITE. HE GETS UP AND LOOKS AT THE DRAWINGS AROUND HIM. ALL OF THE PICTURES AND HIEROGLYPHICS IN THE GRAVE HAVE IMPORTANT MEANINGS. BUT HIS BIRDS MEAN THAT HE LOVED HIS GRANDAD. AND THAT IS THE MOST IMPORTANT THING.

When Angus woke up the next morning, Dummie's bed was empty. Angus jumped up in shock. "Dummie!"

"I am ghere!" Dummie called from the balcony. He came in and smiled, baring his brown teeth. "I know something," he grinned. "Something we will see today. Something nice. Is surprise."

"A surprise? What kind?" Angus asked.

"I ghave seen in dream. We gho see in Sakkara. But I won't say what."

"Is it in your grandad's pyramid?"

"Yes. But I won't tell!"

Angus quickly got dressed. Luckily Dummie wasn't sad anymore, and it made him feel happy too. A surprise? He wanted to know what it was!

They ate in the breakfast room. They had just finished when Mr Greystone came in. "I've already dropped Dimitri at school," he said. "You want to go to Sakkara, don't you? A group of Dutch people from the hotel are going to the burial ground. I've arranged for us to go with them in the bus. Then we'll have a guide."

"A group of Dutch people?" Angus gave his father a shove.

"Well, erm... that's not necessary," said Nick. "We mainly want to go to Sadihotep's grave."

"You can still do that. But there's so much to see, they said. With a guide you'll be able to see much more."

Angus gave his father another shove, but they couldn't do anything to dissuade Mr Greystone. And so after breakfast they ended up climbing into a bus with a group of tourists. Now they'd have to be even more careful about what they said.

Nick sat down next to Dummie and Angus sat next to Mr Greystone. As the bus tooted through the traffic, Angus thought about the surprise. Something in Sadihotep's grave. Might there be a secret chamber? Or maybe something was hidden there?

They finally left the city and the jolting grew less. Angus looked outside. They were driving along a dusty road toward the south. There were a lot less cars, but instead, oxen and donkeys were walking along the road. The Nile must be close, because the land here was green. And there were people working in the fields and houses were being built all over the place.

After a while, they turned off the road and not long after that, they stopped in a carpark. There were already a number of busses there, and groups of people were walking to a row of tall pillars. As soon as they got out of the bus, at least twenty men in long robes came up to them and tried to sell them stuff. Postcards, figurines, books, scarves, and much more.

"It's normal! Just say CHOKRAN," the guide called out. "CHOKRAN! CHOKRAN!"

"What does that mean ?" Nick asked.

"It means: no, thank you. You don't want anything."

"Oh, but I do want something." Nick opened his wallet and was suddenly surrounded by men, all of them talking at the same time and pushing their wares under his nose.

"Hey, wait a minute. No, no postcards. And I don't like figurines!"

Angus and Dummie watched and laughed as Nick did his best to communicate to the men that he only wanted a map. "Yes, that's a nice scarf. Really. But I don't need a scarf. It's much too warm, mate. Calm down! No!" He finally wrestled himself away from the men, clutching a map of the burial ground.

"Pfff, what a business. No, no more! Cho... erm, chocolate! Chocolate!"

"Chokran," giggled Angus.

"Yes, that's what I meant. Well, goodbye! Look men, over there! New bus! Maybe *they're* cold!"

As the vendors ran over to the new bus, Nick, Angus and Dummie hurried after Mr Greystone and their group.

"There! I know!" cried Dummie excitedly. He pointed to a funny-looking pyramid. It wasn't smooth but made up of square layers that were smaller and smaller as they went up. "Pyramid of Djoser!"

"I know about that one too," Angus said happily. "It's the oldest pyramid in Egypt, Dad. It's called a step pyramid."

"Bit bigger than our kitchen steps, isn't it?" joked Nick.

In front of the pyramid was a square piece of ground covered in rubble and bits and pieces of wall. "There was temple. But is ghone," Dummie said, disappointed. "And ghouses also ghone."

Nick went up to the guide. He told him they'd rather look around on their own and asked the way to Sadihotep's pyramid.

"Why alone? And why Sadihotep?" the guide asked in astonishment. "Not much to see there, you know. There are much nicer things to look at. We'll be visiting some famous graves with lots of chambers filled with beautiful paintings, interesting temple ruins..."

"But we want to go to Sadihotep's pyramid," Nick interrupted.

"Oh. Very well then. We'll go there too then in a bit..."

"No. We want to go now. Erm, choco-thingy," Nick said. "Which means, I'll find it myself."

Angus burst out laughing at the guide's look of surprise.

"It's up to you then," the man said, insulted. He pointed to a spot on the map. "It's that way." To Angus' relief, Mr Greystone said he first wanted to look at the step pyramid and would come and find them later.

"Take your time, the pyramid's unlikely to collapse today," said Nick. He waved and they walked off. Angus looked around, fascinated. Sakkara didn't look like a graveyard at all. It was just a bit of desert with some hills, rocks and ruins. They had to walk along a dusty track, veer to the right a couple of times and turn left once. They passed the remains of constructions and a building that still looked well preserved. There were crumbling pyramids on either side and now and then they'd see guards standing in front of holes. These were the entrances to tombs that had been found. Men were working in a trench. They were carefully hacking away at rocks, putting them in baskets and taking them to a small truck. "They must be looking for new graves," Nick said.

"I ghope they never find," Dummie said. He hurried on. "There. That was not. And that not. That was ghone. And there—" He stopped and grabbed Angus' hand. "There it is," he whispered.

They'd already seen the pyramid on the internet but

Angus was still shocked. Sadihotep's pyramid was no more than a scruffy pile of stones. It could just have easily been a hill. It looked abandoned, and there was no sign at all that a temple or road had once been there.

"He's right, it must be that one," Nick said. "Well, nothing left to collapse there. It's already happened.'

"I hope it's still a bit intact inside," Angus whispered in concern.

Nick nodded. "We're about to find out," he said.

There was a path to the entrance from the track. It was not much more than a hole with a bit of new brick-work and some wooden supports.

They paid the guard and looked at each other.

"Well, here we go then," Nick said.

They climbed down a metal staircase. There were only a couple of steps, but the entranceway was even smaller than the one in Gizeh. At the end of it, another corridor began, like in Gizeh, with a few lamps dotted about. Now even Dummie had to walk bent over.

"Look, Dad, lots of hieroglyphics!" Angus cried.

"Where? Ouch! My head!"

"Ghets bigger soon," Dummie giggled.

"I'll already have a concussion by then," muttered Nick.

The corridor ended in a small bare room. Fortunately you could stand up again. Angus looked around in interest. The walls were damaged but paintings could still clearly been seen in some places. In between them, long rows of hieroglyphics ran from top to bottom.

"Is this the burial chamber?" Angus asked. He couldn't see a sarcophagus anywhere.

"Is ghrave for stuff. Room with ghrave is next."

They bent down and went through another narrow passageway. Nick hit his head again. "Whumpy dumpman. Did they have to build it like this?" he complained.

"But room is nice," said Dummie proudly.

Angus said nothing. He didn't think it was that nice. The room was bare and empty and all the paintings were just as damaged as in the previous room. Here and there, Angus did recognize figures, flowers and animals, but that was all. Imagine being a painter back then, he thought. You might spend weeks under the ground painting and after the pharaoh was buried no one would ever see your work again. What a waste.

"Where's the surprise then?" Angus whispered.

Dummie pulled him along. "In room with coffin, is other way," he said.

They wormed their way back to the other room, climbed through a different narrow opening and then they were in Sadihotep's burial chamber. Angus looked around. This was supposed to be a special room then? It was small and rectangular and Angus didn't see much difference from the other rooms. In front of the back wall, there was an enormous stone sarcophagus which they must have found Sadihotep in. The lid was gone and you could look inside, but of course it was just as empty as the room. There were bits of incomplete paintings on the walls.

"What's the surprise then?" Angus asked impatiently.

Dummie walked over to the stone coffin and looked around. "I don't understand. I don't understand," he said in confusion.

"What don't you understand?"

"I don't understand. Is ghone."

"Has your surprise gone? What was it then?"

Dummie pointed to the wall behind the sarcophagus. "I did drawing there, on wall. I was allowed to do in ghrave. With other painters. I was ghood, my father said. But it has ghone."

Angus walked over to the place Dummie was pointing at. "There are all kinds of drawings there," he said.

"But not mine. I don't see."

"What did it look like?"

"I ghave made three birds," Dummie said. "They are white, with black ghead and bit of wings is also black. Bird in middle ghad wings out, ghe was doing dance. Birds from Nile. Very nice birds, I like.'

"A dancing bird?" Angus walked around the sarcophagus and carefully inspected the wall. If you looked hard you could see rows of hieroglyphics and life-sized drawings of people with animal heads. But they were all just as damaged as in the other rooms and in some places the wall was completely bare.

"Where was it exactly? Do you remember?"

"There. Behind coffin. My drawing was there, on wall. But drawing is ghone. Ghow is possible?"

Angus bit his lip. Again. It was as though they were only having bad luck. Now of all of things, there was nothing left of Dummie's drawing.

Dummie suddenly grabbed Angus' hand. "Angus, I think wall is ghone as well!"

"Huh? What do you mean?"

"Wall with drawing is ghone. Behind coffin was bigger. But now not. Is smaller."

"Are you sure?" Angus said doubtfully.

"Yes, of course I know. I ghave seen it!"

Dummie walked over to the wall behind the sarcophagus and gave it a push.

"Hey, don't do that, the place will collapse," Nick cried in fright. "Maybe your drawing is just in a different room."

Dummie shook his head. "I made drawing of birds

on wall in big room, behind ghrave. Ghepsetsut said I could. But room is different. And drawing is ghone."

He took a few steps away from the wall and towards the coffin. "I was not ghere. Not possible, this. I don't know anymore..." He turned around sadly and walked towards the hole leading to the first room.

"What do you think, Dad?" Angus whispered.

"That he's mistaken. He was only about five or six years old. Maybe it was a different room."

"But he says the entire wall has gone."

"Well, I can see a wall there," Nick said drily.

"But... could they have built an extra wall? Maybe they built a secret room after the funeral, one he doesn't know about. Is that possible?"

Nick shook his head. "He's confused. There was no wall and there was no drawing. Once a pyramid has been closed up, they never open it again."

Angus went back to the first room, disappointed. He went back into the empty treasure room and carefully studied all the drawings. But there wasn't a dancing bird anywhere to be seen. Dummie kept on pacing up and down and shaking his head.

"Ghere was room for treasure, ghere was for ghods and ghere was ghrave room with my drawing. I know for sure," he said for the third time. "Wall is really ghone." And with a sigh, "Everything is ghone."

"Aha, there you are," they suddenly heard Mr Greystone say. "Well, this is all rather basic. Just nearby there's a tomb with much nicer drawings. Do you want to see that one?"

Angus looked at his father.

"I want to get out of here," Nick said.

"Alright, we'll be with you soon," Angus said.

Nick disappeared after Mr Greystone into the passageway and hit his head yet again on the ceiling. "Whumpy, whumpy ten times dumpman!" he shouted crossly.

Angus was unable to laugh. He walked over to Dummie, who had sat down on the floor with his fingers around his scarab. He looked at his friend. What could he say? And Dummie had stopped talking too. The silence was simply awful.

After a long time, Dummie stood up and they clambered back out in silence. Nick was standing outside in the shade next to the entrance. He had decided to wait for them. By now he was drenched in sweat and had at least a hundred bumps on his head, he said.

They went into another tomb a little further along and found the group with Mr Greystone. The guide was telling them all about graves, hieroglyphics, drawings and gods. But Angus barely looked. And Dummie was completely silent. He walked quietly past the most beautiful drawings and said nothing.

Finally the group returned to the bus. It was only midday, but no one had the energy to stay any longer. Mr Greystone wanted to do a bit of work, Nick was too hot, and Dummie just trailed along after them without speaking. What they had been trying to tell him the whole time had probably sunk in: that everything had gone.

Angus stopped in front of the bus. "Dad, Dummie,

shouldn't we stay and look for Akhnetut's grave?" he asked quietly. "That's what we came for, isn't it?"

"No, I don't want," said Dummie.

"Huh? Why not?"

"I won't find," Dummie said listlessly.

Angus was shocked. Was Dummie giving up? "Dummie! You said you'd find it."

"No. Everything is ghone," Dummie said sadly. "My ghome is no more. Ghrave of Akhnetut is maybe ghone too. Or broken. Ghone. Everything ghone."

He turned around and got into the bus after the group of people.

Angus looked at Dummie's drooping shoulders and felt a stab of pain in his stomach, he was so sorry for him. "Do something, Dad," he pleaded.

"I don't know what to do," Nick said. "He's right. Maybe I don't want him to find it anymore either."

"Yes, but this! This is so sad, isn't it?"

"Yes. It's terrible. We should never have come," Nick said quietly.

They got into the bus and drove back to the hotel in silence.

Since Dummie kept on insisting the wall had gone, they looked at the map of the pyramid in the hotel again.

"It's completely right," said Nick.

"But it is not. Wall with drawing is ghere," Dummie said miserably. He pointed at the map.

Nick shrugged uncomprehendingly and Dummie disappeared onto the balcony.

"Dad, it is a bit strange that he's saying a whole wall

has gone, isn't it?" Angus whispered.

"The wall hasn't gone," Nick said.

"Why's he saying it then?"

"He's disappointed. He simply can't believe his drawing is not there. So he's saying the whole wall has gone instead," said Nick.

"But where have the birds gone then?"

"That's what I'm saying. Nowhere. There wasn't any drawing of birds. He dreamed it. You dream things sometimes too, don't you? And then you wake up and it wasn't real."

"But his other dreams were real."

"Dreams are strange things inside your head," Nick said, shaking his. "Some things are based on reality and other things aren't. Your brain just does its own thing when you're asleep."

Angus sighed. "So there never was a drawing."

"No," Nick said.

"What now?"

Nick sighed even deeper. "I don't know either," he said.

They didn't do anything for the rest of the afternoon. Dummie sat on the balcony staring into space and Nick went to read on his bed. Angus picked up a book too but was unable to take in a word.

Around six o'clock, Mr Greystone knocked on the door.

"Did you see a lot of things this afternoon?" he asked cheerfully. Then he saw their miserable faces. "What's the matter?"

"It's hot and we've seen so much it's made us grumpy," Nick lied. "Have you got any ideas to cheer us up? Old music perhaps? Or something from the past they still have now?"

Angus looked up. This was clever of his father. Old music, Dummie might like that. But you'd have to be a super-clown to cheer Dummie up.

"Alright then, I'll sort something out," Mr Greystone promised. He went away and returned ten minutes later with a big smile on his face, and Dimitri. "They had a good idea at Reception. We're going out," he said cheerfully. "I've booked a table at a special restaurant. It'll be quite an experience."

"What kind?" Angus asked.

"Wait and see," Mr Greystone said with a wink.

The restaurant was close to the hotel and they went there by foot. Dummie still didn't say a word. Angus took his hand and didn't let go. As long as Dummie wasn't saying anything, he felt just as miserable himself. But maybe the old music would help a bit.

The restaurant looked more like a theatre than a place to eat. There were tables around a stage and they sat down in the middle at the front. The two Dutch men from the hotel had had the same idea, because they came in just after then and picked a table further along. The tall man looked over at them and waved. The short man turned his back to them. Maybe he didn't feel like seeing other Dutch people either.

Mr Greystone ordered dishes for the whole table. "Leave everything to me tonight," he said jovially. "We're going to have typical Egyptian food today. Can we get anything at all to eat for Dummie?"

"No. He's just eaten," said Nick.

The restaurant slowly filled up. They were brought tea and a while later, the first dishes arrived. Nick pulled a face as he looked at the strange green puree, something rolled up in leaves, and pieces of grilled meat with bones sticking out of them. "No broccoli today either," he muttered. He reluctantly spread some of the green stuff on a slice of bread and cautiously bit into it. His expression changed. "It's delicious!"

"It's chickpea puree," Mr Greystone chuckled. "So you still get your greens. Because of the peas! Kgrrr! Kgrrr! Don't eat too much, Dimitri. You never know!"

Suddenly the lights went out and a couple of spot-lights came on. It grew silent. Everyone stopped eating and stared expectantly at the stage.

An old man appeared from the wings carrying a stool. He was wearing nothing but green baggy trousers and there was a rolled up cloth on his head. He put down the stool, fetched a basket and carefully put it on the floor. Then he pulled out a pipe, calmly took the lid off the basket and sat down. Then he slowly began to play.

Angus looked at Dummie in disappointment. Sad music like that wouldn't cheer anyone up. But to his surprise, Dummie grabbed his arm. "I know!" he cried. "I know what is in!"

"What?"

"Look!" As the man moved the pipe back and forth, a snake's head suddenly appeared from out of the basket. The snake slowly rose up and made its neck wider. Its body swayed back and forth.

"This is dangerous snake!" cried Dummie. "If ghe bite you, you die!"

Angus stared in shock as the snake's head rose higher and higher.

"Dad, how big are those snakes? Dad? Why are you standing up, Dad?"

"I'm checking where the emergency exit is," Nick whispered as he sat back down.

Angus burst into nervous laughter.

"Yeah, you know, that creature might turn nasty. Having that irritating piping around its head the whole time."

"Cobras are deaf," Mr Greystone whispered. "They move in time with the pipe moving. They're actually upset and want to flee."

"Oh, even better!" Nick said with a grimace. "They'd better not flee into the audience."

The snake charmer stood up and the cobra rose higher still. Angus paid close attention, the snake was indeed copying the pipe's movements. How did the man manage to play it so calmly! It was terrifying.

After a while the man sat back down again. The snake swayed lower and lower and finally disappeared into the basket. The charmer put the lid on, stood up and bowed. The room was filled with thunderous applause. The lights went back up and as Nick leaned back in his chair in relief, new dishes were brought to the table.

"That man is magic!" laughed Dummie. "Is very ghood! Is from my country."

Angus smiled at him in relief. The snake had gone and Dummie had spoken again.

Ten minutes later the lights went out for the second time. Cheerful music blared through the room. A moment later, ten dancers appeared, followed by musicians with tambourines and some strange instruments. They were all wearing baggy trousers and vests covered in glitter and little bells.

From one moment to the next, the room was filled with yells and cheers.

Dummie grabbed hold of Angus. "I know as well!" he shouted. "Dancing was in temple. And at Dad's party. Everywhere. I know it! It is ghood!"

He stood up and began to clap very loudly.

The dancers whooped and leaped around. Then they stood in a row and began to belly dance. The little bells jingled faster and faster.

"I can too!" Dummie cried. He leapt from his chair and before Angus could stop him, he'd climbed onto the stage and joined the dancers. He held his hands in the air and began to waggle his belly hilariously. The dancers cheered and clapped and formed a row behind him.

Dimitri waved his cap, laughing hysterically and Mr Greystone could hardly control himself either. "Hahaha, look at him! Kgrrr! Kgrrr! Kgrrr!"

Everyone in the room laughed and clapped for that crazy little fellow with the bandages around his head who was dancing even more wildly than the men with the bells.

Suddenly one of the dancers gestured to Dummie to lift his T-shirt.

"Blasting cackdingle. They want to see his belly!" said Angus, taken aback. To his dismay, Dummie didn't hesitate for a second but took off his T-shirt. The room suddenly fell silent. "Oooh," people murmured. And then there was whispering. Angus quickly looked around but nobody started to scream. Apparently everyone thought that Dummie had had a terrible accident and they all felt sorry for him. Dummie bowed. Then he waved, picked up what looked like a tambourine and began to shake it merrily. There was relieved applause from the crowd.

Now all the dancers surrounded Dummie and gestured for him to take the lead. Dummie began to dance more and more energetically, jumping in the air, sinking to the floor and doing pirouettes. The crowd were splitting their sides because the dancers couldn't even keep up!

Suddenly Angus noticed a brown stripe on Dummie's back. He squinted to get a better look. In horror he watched as a strip of the white bandage begin to sag, revealing Dummie's own brown bandages. Nick saw it too. "There, on his back! He's about to turn into a real mummy!" he shouted in Angus' ear in panic.

Angus didn't hesitate and ran onto the stage. He stood behind Dummie, put his hands around his waist and began to dance. As the cheers grew even louder, he screamed into Dummie's ear, "Stop! Your bandage is falling off on your back! We have to stop!" But Dummie

didn't hear him. At his wit's end, Angus grabbed hold of Dummie even tighter. Whatever happened now, he'd stay behind Dummie. It was almost impossible because Dummie twisted and turned even more nimbly than that deaf snake.

Angus felt more and more dizzy but he didn't let go. The brown patch got wider and wider until – to make matters worse – a whole strip of bandage came loose and grew longer and longer. It was all about to go horribly wrong.

"You have to stop!" screamed Angus.

After an eternity, the music stopped. Deafening cheers rose from the crowd.

Dummie bowed and Angus bowed over his back. "Put on your T-shirt!" he hissed. "Now!" Dummie picked up his T-shirt and returned to their table. Many people touched him and smiled as he passed.

"I am very ghood," he laughed. And then finally he pulled his T-shirt back over his head.

Angus sunk into his chair. His head was still spinning from all the turning. He leaned back, feeling slightly sick.

"Kgrrr! Kgrrr! Soapy sludgeball!" Mr Greystone roared. "You were fantastic! Doesn't it hurt with all those burns?"

"I feel nothing!" Dummie cried proudly. "Dancing from my country is nice!" He was completely happy again and talked his head off about dancing at parties and in temples and at pharaohs' funerals.

Luckily new dishes of food arrived that Mr Greystone

found so delicious he was immediately distracted. "Look, Nick, mini cupcakes. They are so sweet the fillings jump out of your back teeth. You have to try one. And this one. This is with honey. And those are good too—"

Nick obediently ate one cake after the next, until he was almost bursting, he said.

The waiters cleared the table and then it was over. They paid, got up and cheerfully walked back to the hotel.

Dummie continued to laugh. "Dancing in my country is very nice! Is very nice! Very nice!" he kept saying.

They had almost reached the hotel when the two Dutch men suddenly appeared and joined them. "You're a very good dancer, kid. We laughed ourselves sick," the short man said in a friendly voice. "Are you enjoying Egypt?"

"Well, speaking of sick," Nick said with some difficulty. "I'm not feeling too good."

"That's because of all those cakes," Mr Greystone grinned. "As long as you feel better by tomorrow."

"Oh? What's happening tomorrow?" the short man asked.

"Sakkara again," Nick replied. "There's so much to see there. And what about you?"

"We'll see. Good night then." And suddenly they'd gone.

"Funny fellows, those Dutch people," Nick said.

"You're funny yourself," laughed Mr Greystone.

"Well, it's still true then, isn't it?" giggled Angus.

In the hotel they went straight to the lifts and not long after that, they were back in their room.

"Did you like it?" Nick asked Dummie.

"Very ghood! My ghome is still ghere!" Dummie beamed.

"Great. And now I'm going to wrap you up again." Nick cut off all the loose bandages, got some new rolls and wrapped Dummie back up again tightly.

Just before they'd finished, Dummie began to belly dance again and he had to start over. Nick could get really grumpy about this kind of thing back home, but today he didn't say anything and Angus could understand why.

When they were done, Angus sprayed Dummie with toilet freshener and they went to bed.

The three of them were all so tired, they fell asleep instantly.

DARWISHI IS WALKING ALONG BETWEEN HIS FATHER AND HEPSETSUT IN SAKKARA. THEY PASS THE ENORMOUS STEP PYRAMID AND CLIMB THE HILLS ON THEIR WAY TO SADIHOTEP'S PYRAMID.

WHEN THEY ARE NEARLY THERE, THEY DON'T TURN LEFT TO GRANDAD'S TEMPLE DUT WALK PAST IT, FURTHER INTO THE DESERT.

"WHERE ARE WE GOING?" DARWISHI ASKS IN SURPRISE.

"I WANT TO SHOW YOU SOMETHING," SAYS HEPSETSUT.

HEPSETSUT LEADS THE WAY AND CLIMBS UP ONTO A SMALL PLATFORM THAT IS HIGHER THAN THE REST. THE TOP OF THE PLATFORM IS SLIPPERY. THEY PAUSE IN BETWEEN TWO DEEP CREVICES.

AKHNETUT POINTS AT THE LARGE MASS OF ROCKS NEARBY. "THAT'S WHERE THEY'LL BUILD MY PYRAMID, SON," HE SAYS. "RIGHT NOW, BLOCKS ARE ALREADY BEING CARVED IN OUR QUARRIES A LONG WAY UPSTREAM OF THE NILE. I WILL HAVE THE WORKERS START NEXT TIME IT FLOODS."

"BUT YOU'VE ONLY JUST BECOME KING," DARWISHI SAYS, CONCERNED. "YOU WON'T BE NEEDING A GRAVE FOR A LONG TIME, WILL YOU?"

"DO YOU KNOW HOW LONG IT TAKES TO BUILD A PYRAMID?" HEPTSETUT SMILES.

"QUITE A LONG TIME," DARWISHI SAYS, RELUCTANTLY. IT WASN'T NICE TO START THINKING ABOUT THAT NOW....

HEPSETSUT PICKS UP A FLAT STONE. HE USES A SHARPER STONE TO SCRATCH A MAP ONTO ITS SURFACE. "WE'RE STANDING AT THIS CROSS," HE SAYS. "YOUR PYRAMID WILL HAVE FOUR ROOMS, A TEMPLE AND A STRAIGHT ROAD TO THE NILE, WITH LIONS ON EITHER SIDE."

AKHNETUT SMILES. "FIVE ROOMS," HE SAYS.

"ALRIGHT, FIVE," HEPSETSUT DECIDES.

"CAN I DO A DRAWING IN IT, LIKE IN SADIHOTEP'S GRAVE?" DARWISHI ASKS.

"WHAT DO YOU THINK? YOU CAN DO AS MANY DRAWINGS AS YOU WANT," HIS FATHER LAUGHS.

DARWISHI NODS PROUDLY. OF COURSE HIS FATHER

WILL BUILD THE BIGGEST PYRAMID. AND WHEN HE IS
KING HIMSELF, HE'LL BUILD AN EVEN BIGGER ONE.
MAYBE BEHIND THE BIG ROCK. MAYBE EVEN BIGGER
THAN CHEOPS'S BIG PYRAMID AT GIZEH.

"CAN WE START DIGGING THIS YEAR?" AKHNETUT
ASKS.

"SURE," SAYS HEPSETSUT. "AND NEXT YEAR WE'LL
LAY THE FIRST STONES."

HEPSETSUT PUTS THE FLAT STONE BACK DOWN ON
THE GROUND.

AS HE AND AKHNETUT SET OFF, DARWISHI QUICKLY
HIDES THE STONE IN ONE OF THE FISSURES IN THE
ROCK. WHEN HIS FATHER'S PYRAMID IS FINISHED, HE
WILL TAKE IT OUT AGAIN AND SEE WHETHER
HEPSETSUT REALLY DID MANAGE TO THINK UP
SOMETHING SO COMPLICATED THIS FAR IN ADVANCE.

THEN HE RUNS AFTER THEM, BACK TO SADIHOTEP'S
TEMPLE.

"Angus! Angus!"

Angus shot up in bed. Dummie was sitting next to
him, his golden eyes glowing.

"What is it?" he whispered with a start.

"I ghad dream again," Dummie said excitedly.

Angus blinked. "About the procession? Or your
drawing?"

"No. I know where ghrave of Akhnetut is!"

"What?" Angus was wide awake immediately. "Where then?"

"Just near Sadihotep's pyramid. I dream I am standing on ghill and my father points. Ghe points to place near desert, I am sure. I want to gho back."

"Where is it exactly? Can you draw it? Hang on. Where's that map?" Angus got out of bed, turned on the light and looked for the map of Sakkara on the table.

"What's going on?" asked Nick sleepily. "What time is it?"

"Middle of the night," Angus said hurriedly. "But wake up, Dad. Dummie says he knows where Akhnetut's grave is! Here, the map."

Dummie opened up the map and ran his finger over it.

"Ghere is pyramid of Sadihotep," he said. "I stand on ghill, with my dad, behind me is pyramid of Djoser." He let his finger glide further, hesitated and then went back. "No, I stand ghere. Or ghere, I don't know for sure." He shook his head and began again. "Maybe I stand there. My dad points. Ghe says my ghrave comes there. Next to big pile of rocks."

"Where is that? Just near your grandad's pyramid?" Angus asked excitedly.

"Little bit further. Ghe was ghoing to build pyramid with five rooms. Must be there."

"Oh," said Angus in disappointment. "But your father doesn't have a pyramid, remember?"

"I know. But ghe said I make ghrave there. Must be there. I know for sure."

Nick went to the toilet and teetered back.

"Shall we talk some more tomorrow? I don't feel too good," he groaned.

"But this is important, Dad! He might be right!"

"Yes, maybe," Nick said. "But don't get your hopes up. Dummie was wrong about that drawing too."

"I know for sure!" Dummie said indignantly.

"Yes. And I know for sure that the grave won't walk away in the night. Dummie, if you're right, that's fantastic. But I must sleep now. I don't feel very well. We'll go there tomorrow."

He got back into bed and rolled over. Dummie and Angus stared at the map for a while longer. From time to time, Dummie was absolutely certain, then he'd shake his head again.

"We'll just have to go and look tomorrow," Angus said at last. "We'll look for the hill you were standing on with your dad and then..."

"And then we find my father's ghrave," grinned Dummie.

Angus was silent. He wasn't so sure. His father could be right and it might be like the bird drawing. Your head does strange things when you're dreaming, some things are real and some things aren't, Nick had said. Maybe this wasn't real either. Or it was, both were possible.

They went back to bed and turned out the light. Angus couldn't get back to sleep. Imagine if Dummie was right. Maybe they'd find something! What would happen then? And what would happen if, once again, they didn't find anything at all?

CHAPTER 6
A Cave in the Desert

The next day something terrible happened. Back home, Angus, Nick and Mr Scribble had thought of all kinds of things that could go wrong. Dummie might be found out and they might not be able to find Akhnetut's grave. But what happened that day was something nobody had thought of beforehand.

The day started all wrong.

Angus was woken up by the toilet flushing, three times in a row. After the third time, Nick came out of the bathroom looking pale and flopped onto his bed. "I don't feel very well," he complained. "I've spent the whole night on the toilet."

"We're not flying again until Saturday, remember," Angus joked.

"Shut up. I think it's got something to do with that green stuff. That chickpea gloop. Or it's the pharaoh's curse. I can't do anything today."

Dummie looked up. "You do something. Today we gho back to pyramid of Sadihotep," he said.

"Son, I just can't. I'd cover the whole pyramid in poo. And the bus we'd be taking to get there. I can't leave the hotel today."

Angus looked at his ashen face in disappointment. "But... what about Dummie's dream then?"

"You can... Oh, wait a minute," Nick said as he rushed to the toilet again. When he returned, he was even paler.

"Blasting cackdingle! Why do you always get sick at the most inconvenient times?!" Angus cried angrily. "When Dummie's scarab was stolen, you broke your leg, and now you've got diarrhea! Couldn't you have got that at home?"

"We eat broccoli at home," Nick groaned, clutching his belly.

"Dad, we have to go to Sakkara," Angus said.

"How then? The pyramids won't have toilets,"

"Never mind," said Angus crossly. "So what now?"

"Now I've got cramps," Nick said unhappily.

Angus was really angry. His father might not be able to help it, but it was still his fault. Angus had had to do everything on his own, since the start of their holiday already!

He went down to the breakfast room with Dummie, feeling annoyed. Mr Greystone was there, sitting alone at a table. "Dimitri's ill," he said.

"Oh, my dad is too," Angus said. "Something in the food disagreed with him, he said. He can't get away from the toilet. You should smell it in there. I had to pinch my nose to brush my teeth." This did make them laugh, despite everything.

Suddenly Angus had an idea. "We wanted to go back to Sakkara today, for Dummie's project on Sadihotep. Would you like to come with us? Then Dimitri and Nick can stay here together. They can look after each other and play Pass the Toilet Roll." He winked at Dummie. Mr Greystone found Sadihotep's pyramid boring. He'd surely rather go to a different tomb. If they handled things well, he and Dummie would be able to look around together. In fact, it was a fantastic idea. And Mr Greystone thought so too. "Let's do that then. Has Nick already taken any pills?" he asked.

"What kind of pills?'

"You can get them at the reception. They've got anti-diarrhea pills. Almost everyone gets sick here. It lasts about two days. I'll get him a few."

After they'd eaten, they went back upstairs and luckily Nick thought it was a good idea too. He didn't mind looking after Dimitri if Mr Greystone was happy to look after Angus and Dummie.

The five of them went down to the lobby. Nick gave Angus and Dummie one of the hotel's cards each and some money for if anything happening. "And here's a rucksack with two bottles of water." And then he repeated that they should be careful.

"Yes, Dad, I've been doing that the whole holiday already," Angus said.

"Oh yes, so where's your hat then?" Nick asked. "You'll get sunstroke if you're not careful and then you won't be able to look after me."

"Oops, forgot it," grinned Angus.

Mr Greystone took the cap from Dimitri's head. "Here, take this then," he said.

And then finally they could go.

As they left the hotel, Mr Greystone turned around. "Have you got any pegs?"

"Pegs?" Nick asked foolishly.

"For the stench. And erm... keep the windows closed or all of Cairo will faint. Kgrrr! Kgrrr! Kgrrr!"

"Yes, you go and laugh at our expense," Nick muttered. "Boys, look after that money, and if you get fed up with that pig over there, just take a taxi."

Not long after that, they were driving out of the city. On the way, they discussed what they wanted to do. Angus was completely right – Mr Greystone wasn't interested in going back to Sadihotep's pyramid at all. "If you two promise to stay together, I'll go visit a more interesting tomb," he said. "And if we can't find each other we will meet at the step pyramid at two o'clock, alright?"

"Alright," said Angus and Dummie at the same time.

They got out and walked over to the burial ground. The three of them walked past the step pyramid towards Sadihotep's. Mr Greystone turned left and Dummie and Angus turned right, and then they were alone. "We don't even have a watch," laughed Angus. He looked around. It was already hot and busy. There were tourists everywhere and groups with guides. They passed two men with dromedaries, who gestured at them in a friendly way. Did they want a ride?

"CHOKRAN! CHOKRAN!" giggled Angus. They carried on, took a few turns and then they found themselves at the collapsed pyramid again. Dummie climbed some way up it and looked around. "I think rocks is there," he said, pointing at the hill in front of the desert. But when they got there, Dummie changed his mind.

So they trudged on to a different hill. Angus was feeling hot again, Dimitri's cap was sticking to his head like a warm pancake. It wasn't the next hill either, nor the one after that. They walked back and started again. At each hill, Dummie shook his head. Angus could understand. There wasn't anything to see. And everything looked the same, too. His spirits sagged. "I don't believe..." he began.

"There!" cried Dummie. "I know! There I stood. I see ghood!" He pointed at a pile of rocks. "Behind me is pyramid of Sadihotep. I walk ghere with Gheptsetut and my Dad. I know for sure!"

They began to run together. They climbed up the rocks and paused, panting. Dummie pointed to the flat top of the rocks they were standing on. "I know sure. Ghere was strange flat rock." Dummie said. "Then my dad pointed there. Ghe say, 'My pyramid will come there.'"

"Where is it exactly?" Angus asked excitedly.

"There, close by! Near big rock with stones," Dummie pointed.

"Are you sure?"

"Yes. Then Ghepsetsut takes small stones... Wait! I

know again!" Dummie took a couple of steps backwards, bent over and stuck his hand into a gash in the rocks. He triumphantly pulled out a thin, flat stone. "MAASHI! MAASHI!" he shrieked.

Angus took the stone from Dummic's hand. He couldn't see anything special, just a few scratches.

"This is drawing!" Dummie said. "Ghepsetsut made drawing of ghrave. Drawing is top view. Ghere is temple! And Nile. And cross is us now."

Blasting cackdingle! Now Angus could see it too. There were some small squares and lines next to a large square. "Did Ghepsetsut do this? So it's been here for more than four thousand years? And no one has ever seen it? No, I don't believe it!"

"No one looked there. And you didn't see it too," said Dummie.

Angus' heart began to beat faster. "Alright, let's see. Then it must be... there." He pointed at the rocky outcrop that Dummie had also pointed at.

"MAASHI. That is," Dummie grinned. Suddenly he grabbed the stone from Angus' hand and smashed it so hard onto the ground that it burst into pieces.

"Hey? What are you doing?" Angus said in shock.

"I break stone. Is no longer needed."

"But it's of your father's grave!"

"No one must find," Dummie said. "Come on!"

They ran down the hill towards the rocks. Angus looked back when they were halfway. Sadihotep's pyramid was actually close by, but from this side you could only see the top of it. And that meant that no one could see them, which was good! They cautiously began to circle the rocks. Angus was looking for something manmade. Or a piece of wall perhaps. He stopped at a gash at the back. "Here's something," he exclaimed.

They tiptoed inside and arrived in a dark round space. It looked like a natural cave. In the middle of it was an enormous block, and apart from that just pebbles and sand. They inspected every stone and every nook and cranny together. But there was absolutely nothing that might have been made by people.

"This isn't anything," Angus said in disappointment.

A little bit further along from the cave was another deep recess but it was a dead end.

"Maybe this was the place the grave was supposed to be," Angus guessed. "But your father died after such a short space of time, Mr Scribble said. Maybe he didn't have time for it. They didn't even start." They walked around the walls once again but didn't find anything. It was just an empty cave. Angus thought about what his dad had said. Your mind does funny things in dreams, sometimes it's real and sometimes it's not. But that flat stone with the drawing on it was just as real as his father's stomach ache.

They reluctantly went back outside. Dummie clambered up the rocks to check there. Angus looked at the tip of Sadihotep's pyramid. Mr Greystone was somewhere beyond it. He'd given them two hours. How long had they been away already? Maybe half an hour. A couple of men with dromedaries appeared in the distance. Angus ducked behind the rocks, sat down in the shade, got a bottle of water from his rucksack and reflected.

Suddenly he heard a thud.

Angus froze and pricked up his ears.

"Yoo-hoo!" said a voice. Angus quickly took a sip, put his bottle back in his rucksack and stood up. "I'm coming!" he called.

And then it happened.

Angus went around the corner and found himself staring right into the brown faces of two men in long robes, with scarves around their heads and a rope in their hands. Before he knew it, there was a hand over his mouth and his hands were being tied behind his back.

"Help!" he cried in a muffled voice. He thrashed and kicked for all he was worth. He felt dizzy and began to see stars. He was about to pass out.

With a superhuman effort, he managed to break free. "Dummie!" he screamed. Then he felt a blow to his head and everything went black.

CHAPTER 7
kidnapped

Angus blinked. His head was pounding and his mouth was dry. He cautiously tried to move. A flash of pain shot through his head.

"Oh good, you're awake," said a vaguely familiar voice.

A man's head appeared. To Angus' astonishment, he recognized the tall skinny man from the hotel. But why was his face so brown and why was he wearing a long dress? He opened his mouth to say something and was immediately hit by another flash of pain.

"Where am I?" Angus groaned. His voice sounded hoarse.

"In the desert. In a cave. I'm afraid you'll have to be here for a little while. Sorry," the man said. "But if your father pays, you'll be set free again tomorrow."

"Set free?" Angus tried to get up. Only then did he notice that his hands were tied together. Something chinked and he saw a padlock near his feet. A chain ran from one foot to a large block and there was a padlock on that too.

"I'm trapped! It hurts," he groaned.

"Yes, sorry, Harry was quite clear about that," the man said. "He's the boss, you know." He moved the chain to one side so it would be less in Angus' way. "Sorry, lad, but this is necessary," he apologized. "Harry didn't think a rope would be enough. And I agree actually. Otherwise you might escape. No, not might, *would*."

"But... what's going on? Unchain me."

"No, I can't," the man said. "Sorry, I really am. Here, have a drink. Whaah!" He tripped over his robe and splashed water over Angus. "This stupid disguise!" He clumsily lifted up his skirts and gave Angus a sip of water.

Angus didn't understand any of it. Disguise? Why was the man in disguise? Suddenly a horrible thought occurred to him. "Have I... been kidnapped?"

"Yes, of course. It was Harry's idea. We were actually going to Egypt for a little break. Things had gone wrong with a bank rob— No, I'd better not tell you about that. We simply came here. Just like that. But then we saw you in the airplane. Or we saw you all at the airport, in fact. Harry recognized your father. Kidnapping is easier than robbing a bank. No, I shouldn't say that. All I mean is – if your dad pays, we'll be rich."

Angus closed his eyes. Rob a bank? Kidnapping? Pay? They only had ten thousand euros and they'd nearly used all of it on this trip.

"But my father doesn't have any money," he groaned.

"Mr Greystone has got more than enough money. A

little bit more or less won't make any difference to him."

"But why would Mr Greystone pay for me?"

"Because you're his son, of course!"

Because you're his son! Angus suddenly began to make sense of it. They thought he was Dimitri! "But I'm—" He shut his mouth. He'd almost said the wrong thing. If they thought he was Dimitri, the last thing he should do is say he wasn't! Otherwise he'd be useless to them and they might just leave him here. His chest felt tight. Left alone here without food or drink, he'd die a horrible death. But being kidnapped... What had Dimitri said? That they cut off your little finger?

"Where am I?" he asked anxiously.

"I'm not telling you. You're simply here," the man said. He even began to laugh.

"But... how long have I been here?"

"Hours. You were, um... unconscious. But that wasn't deliberate. Sorry."

"And Dummie? The boy with the burns?"

"Harry hit him too. Sorry. Say...." He looked around in concern. "Maybe you know, I mean... I'm not scared or anything, you know, only, um...." He leaned in towards Angus. "Are there scorpions here?" he whispered.

There was a scraping noise in the distance. Then a bang, footsteps and the light of a torch.

The fat short man from the hotel came into the cave. He also had a brown face and was wearing another of those long robes. "Ted? What are you doing?" he said.

Ted stood up awkwardly. "Hi boss," he said. "Erm, I

looked after him. Did you talk to the millionaire?"

"Everything's fixed. His old man knows about it. I called him on his mobile. Good idea, asking for the number at the hotel. They just gave it to me, ha ha. I told him, 'No police or you'll never see your son again.' You should have heard him panic. Panting away, he was really scared. It might take a while before he can get the money to Egypt. We'll keep the lad here until then."

Angus tried to think clearly. Mr Greystone had understood the muddle and had played along in any case. Pff! His heart was in his throat.

Harry picked up his rucksack. "Ted, come with me," he said.

Angus stiffened. Were they both going to leave?

"Where are you going?" he squeaked.

"None of your business. We have to fix something."

"Hang on, boss. Are there scorpions here? I mean, wouldn't it be better to hide the lad in Cairo? That would be much better. It's so, erm... empty here! He might get bitten. Or I might."

"It's just for a couple of days. We're not going to move the boy. I don't know if Mr Greystone will keep his word. For all you know, the burial ground might be swarming with policemen. Well, come along."

"Wait a minute!" Angus cried in panic. "Don't go! I'm... I'm thirsty."

Ted leaned down and gave him some more to drink.

"Sorry," he whispered. "We'll be back soon."

They walked away, there was a scraping noise and then Angus was alone.

"Help! Help!" cried Angus. "HELP!"

He listened but there was only silence. Angus took a deep breath. He mustn't panic now. The men were coming back. Or they might discover they had the wrong boy and not come back... No, that Ted would come back for sure. He didn't seem so bad. Or was he?

He looked around anxiously. He was lying in a small cave. There was a little bit of light coming from somewhere above, it must be an opening. He tugged at the chain but it wouldn't budge. He couldn't move his hands either. It was already hot and he was feeling hotter and hotter.

"Anybody here? Help!" he shouted.

There was a rustling sound. Angus froze. Was it a scorpion? Or a snake perhaps, one of those cobras? His chest felt tight again. "Kssst! Go away! Kssst!" he squealed. More rustling. Now he screamed. "Aarghh! HELP!'

"Angus!" a voice whispered.

"Dummie!" Angus almost fainted in relief.

"Angus! I am ghere!"

"Where? I can't see you. What happened?"

"Men in desert ghit you and took you. I only saw later. You were already on Dairy."

"Dairy? What's Dairy?"

"Dummy Dairy!" said Dummie.

Angus burst into nervous laughter. "Was I kidnapped on a dromedary?"

"Two Dairies. With little desert man on back."

"Dummie, there aren't desert men. They're the men from the hotel! They're in disguise. They kidnapped me!"

"What is kidnapped?"

"That they take you and hold you prisoner somewhere. They think I'm Dimitri. They want Mr Greystone to pay money and then they'll let me go. Dummie? Dummie? Where are you?"

"I am ghere, in dark," Dummie replied.

"Did you warn Mr Greystone?"

"No. Not possible. I stay with you. I ghave ghidden under other Dummy Dairy. So I could see where you gho. But ghanging on Dummy Dairy went wrong. But I gheld on to rope. They did not see."

"But where are we then?"

"In cave, in desert. I ghid."

"Oh, Dummie, how good of you. Can you undo me?"

To his surprise, Dummie didn't move from where he was.

"What's the matter? Why won't you come closer?"

"Not saying."

"Dummie, undo me!"

"You must close eyes."

"Huh? Why?"

"Because... you can't see me."

"But I know what you look like! Hurry up now."

"I... I am naked."

Angus clamped his mouth shut. "What?"

"Bandage is off. I fall from Dairy. I cannot ghold on, only to rope. I ghave to ghold scarab. And photo thingy. Dummy Dairy drag me over stones."

"Really? Oh, but that must hurt!"

"I feel nothing. But first clothes is ghone, and then bandage broken. Came loose and fell off. Is ghone."

"Your bandages? You mean everything?"

Dummie was silent.

"Dummie, are you completely naked?"

"Yes. You close eyes?"

"And your scarab? Do you still have your scarab?" Angus asked hastily.

"Yes," said Dummie. "On chain on neck."

Angus took a deep breath in relief. "Alright! I don't care what you look like. Undo me!"

"I am scary ugly mummy, like Sadihotep."

"Dummie! Undo me!"

"MAASHI." Dummie took a step forward and come into the light. Dummie had warned him, but Angus still got a horrible fright. Only Dummie's head was still partly bandaged and there was the odd frayed bit of linen here and there. But the rest was gone. Dummie had the same black skin as the mummies in the museum and looked just as horrific. The camera and the scarab hung around his miserably skinny neck.

"Blasting cackdingle," whispered Angus. He closed his eyes. Things were just getting worse and worse. He was chained up and Dummie was naked. It was a disaster.

"Is scary?" Dummie asked.

"Yes. No. It's not that bad," Angus lied. "But it doesn't matter. Undo me!"

"Yes, I do." Dummie came closer. Angus looked at the skin pulled tight across his bones. He thought about what his father had said when Dummie had first come into their home. He had to keep looking at Dummie so that he'd get used to his scary face. It had worked then. But now... Dummie looked awful. His friend was a monster...

Dummie kneeled down and tried to undo the rope around Angus' wrists. He pulled harder and harder but the rope only got tighter. "Can't," he said moodily.

"Cut it. Use something sharp, a stone," Angus suggested.

Dummie looked for a good stone, slashed and scratched with it and ended up cutting Angus' arm. Angus almost threw up. In the meantime, he was listening to check if he couldn't hear anything.

Suddenly the rope shot free.

"Yes! It worked!" cried Angus.

His fingers began to tingle but he didn't have time to think about that. "Now the chain!"

They grabbed the chain and pulled as hard as they could. And again. And yet again. "It'll never work," groaned Angus.

"Will. Gharder!" Dummie braced himself against the wall and pulled with all his might. There was a sudden snap and something fell onto the ground.

"Stop!" screamed Angus. "You're falling apart!"

Dummie looked in shock at the piece of skin that had fallen off his arm.

Angus almost panicked. Lots of bits of skin were hanging off Dummie. He might fall apart completely! "You have to put something on," he cried. "You have to. Look there! The clothes belonging to those men." He pointed to a corner of the cave where a pile of clothes was next to a couple of coils of rope. "Put those on. Now! I insist!'

Dummie walked over to the pile and pulled out a pair of trousers and a shirt. The clothes were much too big, but Angus rolled up the trouser legs and the sleeves and quickly wrapped two whole coils of rope around Dummie. He could breathe again. Not their problems were any less, but now he didn't have to worry about Dummie losing bits of his body. But Dummie's hands and face were still bare. He could hardly go and fetch help.

They desperately began to pull again. But the chain didn't budge.

"We're just not strong enough," groaned Angus. He tried to come up with something clever, but it was made his head hurt again.

"I know," Dummie said all of a sudden. "I gho ghet donkey. Donkey is strong."

"A donkey? Where are you going to find a donkey?"

"I find one," said Dummie. "You wait ghere." He got up.

"Dummie, wait a minute! Are there any nasty creatures here? Those snakes?"

"Maybe. Or different animal. Big spider with sting."

"Do you mean a scorpion?"

"Is that spider with sting?"

"How should I know? With its tail up."

"Yes, that is ghere. But ghe do nothing if you don't scare ghim."

"Alright. I'll wait for you. Oh, shhh!" Angus froze. The scraping sound again and footsteps. "Too late! Hide!"

Dummie looked around hastily. To Angus' left was a small recess with no light coming from it.

Dummie rushed over to it, wormed his way in and disappeared.

A moment later, the men came into the cave with two big rucksacks. They took bread and water out of them. Angus quickly held his hands behind his back and used his free leg to kick away the loose bit of rope.

"See, we're back," Ted said. "Sorry we left you alone for so long. But we had to make a phone call. And get bread, and extra torches, and..."

"Stop jabbering and give the boy something to eat," Harry snapped.

"Yes, boss. I will, boss. Of course."

Angus bit into his bread obediently. The thought of food made him feel sick, but if he didn't eat, he'd only get weaker.

"Sorry. Once your father has paid, you'll be free again," Ted whispered uneasily.

Angus took another bite. His mind raced. Dummie had to get out of there. He had to distract the men. If he perhaps.... "Whaah!" he screamed at the top of his voice.

Ted almost fell backwards in shock.

"There, I can see something moving! There! In the corner!"

"What? Where?" Harry grabbed a stone and walked over to the corner. Angus quickly looked back. Dummie had understood, luckily. As the men bent down to look, Dummie crept out of his nook, waved to Angus and quickly ran away.

"I can't see anything! You were having us on."

"Sorry, I thought I saw something," groaned Angus.

"I told you, boss. There are scorpions."

"Of course there are. This is the desert," snarled Harry. "But those things won't hurt you. Only if you make them angry."

"Are you sure?"

"Yes. And now stop making me angry!"

Ted sat back down again. "Sorry, boss. I don't like those creatures. Did you see that snake in the restaurant? They've got them here too. And god knows what else there is. I can't bear this desert. It might freeze tonight too. It freezes at night in the desert. I heard that once."

"Perfect, then we can go ice-skating tomorrow," Harry said drily.

"Skating? But there's no water!"

"Oh shut up, you idiot."

Harry picked up a chunk of bread and began to eat.

"Harry?"

"Yeeees?"

"Do you think he's going to pay?"

"Leave that to me."

"But what if he doesn't pay?" Ted asked.

"Of course he'll pay. It's his son!" Harry said.

"He does look a bit like that other boy."

"The other one's got a hat. I'm not stupid enough to kidnap the wrong boy."

"No, you're not," Ted mumbled.

There was a moment's silence.

"If he doesn't pay, we're stuck with the boy," Ted began again. "Wouldn't it just have been better to rob Mr Greystone?"

"Kidnapping his son is much more lucrative. Well, Ted. You don't have to be part of this, you know."

"I do, I do," Ted said quickly. "But isn't kidnapping for criminals?"

"And what are we then?"

Ted was quiet as though he was thinking about it. "Well, just thieves?" he said then.

"Exactly. And now it's time for the big job. Running into Mr Greystone was a stroke of luck. And me recognizing him! And him having his son with him too. And no bodyguards. It can't be a coincidence, us meeting him. It was simply meant to be."

"Oh? Who meant it to be then?" Ted asked.

"Oh, shut up. Just do what I say. In a couple of days we'll be rich and we won't have to steal anymore."

There was another silence.

"Harry?"

"What now?"

"How are you going to get the money?"

"He has to put it in a bin bag and leave it at the carpark near the big pyramids."

"They'll have people watching, won't they?"

"No, he won't dare. He won't get his son back until we've left the country. I'll call him from the airport with the hiding place. And if he calls the police, that'll be the end of his son." Angus stiffened.

"What? I don't want that!" Ted cried. "We wouldn't do that, would we?"

"No, of course not. But he doesn't know that, does he? It's all been a piece of cake so far. Kidnapping is much easier than you think. And everything's been working to our advantage. Those boys going treasure hunting in the desert...

"Treasure hunting? Is there any treasure here?"

"No. Just more graves."

"Oh, grave-hunting," Ted said foolishly.

"Oh, shut up."

Harry got up and went back over to Angus. "Won't be long before we're rich, eh young Greystone?"

"My father will find you," Angus said bravely.

"No, he won't. Your father will pay."

"And what if he doesn't? You're not going to cut off my little finger, are you?" Angus couldn't help himself, it just slipped out.

"No, of course not," cried Ted. "Will we, Harry?"

Harry grinned. "I was thinking more like a tuft of hair," he said.

"Hee-haw! Hee-haw!" rang out in the distance.

Angus jumped.

"I can hear a donkey," Ted said.

"So what? There are lots of them around here. What are you doing?"

"I keep tripping over this stupid dress all the time. I look like a monk. I'm looking for my clothes. They were here."

"You're always losing everything."

"Yes, but I could swear..."

"Hee-haw! Hee-haw!"

"Go and have a look," Harry commanded in irritation.

Ted looked around one last time and then went over to the entrance. He soon came back.

"Can't see anything," he said. "Sorry, Harry. It's making me nervous."

"That's because we didn't get any sleep last night. Here, a sleeping bag. We'll go to sleep and take turns being the look-out. You can start."

Ted got into the sleeping back.

"You can start as the look-out!" Harry barked.

"Sorry." With a sigh, Harry got out of the sleeping bag again. "I'm tired too," he complained.

"That's why you need to go to sleep in a bit," Harry said.

"OK, boss. Thanks."

"Shut up."

"OK. Sorry."

As Harry curled up in his sleeping bag, Ted sat down on the ground. After a while, he walked over to Harry and checked whether he was asleep. He tiptoed over to one of the rucksacks, got a bottle out of it, opened it and took a big gulp. Then he saw Angus watching.

"It helps with the nerves," he said. "Yes, I'm sorry, I'm really nervous." He put the bottle back again, changed his mind and then sat leaning against the wall with the bottle. He took a few more sips. "It wasn't my idea, you know. But Harry's the boss. He says he's cleverer than me. You know what?" He took another sip. "He is too. I'm a bit scared of him sometimes. Once your father has paid, I'm going to get away from him."

Angus took a deep breath. That Ted really wasn't very clever. Maybe he could try something.

"Ted, can I ask you something?"

"Yes, sure."

"Where are the keys? To the padlocks?"

"I don't know. Harry hid them. He doesn't trust me. Hey, why do you want to know?" he asked suspiciously.

"My leg's getting sore."

Ted staggered over and looked at the chain.

"Sorry. I'm really sorry." He sat down again and took another sip.

"It really does help," he muttered. He slowly sank to one side. Five seconds later, he began to snore.

Angus listened. It was totally quiet, apart from the snoring. No donkey sounds any more either. Had Dummie forgotten how to find them? What if he was lost in the desert? He started to sweat again.

Then Dummie appeared in front of him so unexpectedly that he almost screamed in fright.

"Dummie!" he whispered. "Oh, Dummie, shhh." He laid a finger over his lips and pointed at the sleeping men. Dummie immediately picked up a rock and tiptoed over to them. "I will ghit them," he hissed.

"No! Nooo! I'd still be chained up. They've hidden the keys. I want to get out of here. Where's the donkey? Don't hit them!"

Dummie hesitated. "OK. Donkey is outside," he whispered then. He picked up a new coil of rope and fastened it quietly around the chain. "I gho. I fix rope to donkey. Donkey pulls chain and it breaks."

"Or I do," Angus said in alarm.

"No, I do ghood." Dummie took the end of the rope, waved and disappeared.

Angus looked at the two men uneasily. By the looks of it, they were fast asleep. But if they woke up suddenly, he'd be in trouble.

The rope began to move next to the chain. It slowly tightened. It began to shake.

Angus held his breath. Suddenly he felt a tug. And another one. He anxiously checked each link in the chain. Yes, there! One link was slightly open. Another tug and the link opened a bit more. Come on! Just as long as the rope didn't break. Snap, he thought. Snap now, chain.

The next tug was enormous. With a dull clank, the chain snapped in two. A sharp jab of pain went through Angus' feet and that same moment, he was pulled, chain and all, across the floor of the cave. The metal rang like a doorbell and Angus clamped his teeth together so as not to scream. Before he knew it he was outside. The donkey carried on walking.

"Stop! Stop!" moaned Angus.

Dummie grabbed the reins and finally Angus lay unmoving.

"It worked!" Dummie cried in excitement.

"Yes. And I'm broken," Angus groaned. His back was burning and his eyes filled with tears from the bright sun. He could vaguely see sand, stones, hills and more hills. "Where are we?"

"I know," Dummie said as he quickly untied the rope. He lifted up the piece of chain that was still fastened to Angus' foot. "Put this around belly."

Angus staggered to his feet and obediently wrapped the chain around his waist.

"Now we gho quick," Dummie said. "We gho on donkey." He pulled the donkey along for a short distance so they wouldn't be heard and jumped on to it. "Ghet on back," he ordered. Angus climbed up behind him and clung onto Dummie. This would be over soon. Dummie kicked the donkey's sides. "Ghup ghup," he said. The animal shook its head and remained standing there. "Come on, ghup," Dummie tried. But the donkey shook its head and wouldn't budge an inch.

"Ghet off now," Dummie said impatiently. As soon as they were back on the ground, the animal began to walk. But when they'd got back on again, it stopped dead in its tracks again.

Ghup

Angus felt like screaming. Now he'd escaped and the stupid animal wouldn't cooperate!

"The dromedaries!" he suggested. "We'll take the dromedaries!" How silly he hadn't thought of this earlier. If they took the dromedaries the men wouldn't be able to come after them either.

Dummie kept on tugging at the reins, but when the donkey kept on refusing to move and even began to buck, he gave up. "OK. We take the Dairies. But donkey must come too! I won't leave donkey with stupid wusses ghere!"

They ran back to the cave. The dromedaries lay in the sun and looked at them inquisitively. "We'll take one each. Do you know how it works?" Angus asked in a hurry.

"I think just kick it," Dummie said,

They climbed onto the bumps and grabbed the reins. Dummie's dromedary got up at once. But Angus' was as stubborn as the donkey and did nothing. Angus felt even hotter than he already was. They had lost so much time. The men would wake up soon. And if they saw Dummie...

"Come on now!" he screamed into the animal's ear. "Hup hup. Giddy-up! MAASHI! MAASHI!" But whatever he tried, the creature just laid there. "This animal doesn't work!" he shouted.

"Come on my Dairy," Dummie said. Without waiting for an answer, he pulled Angus up behind him and handed him the rope tied to the donkey. Boiling hot, Angus wrapped his arms around Dummie. He hoped that the other dromedary would carry on refusing to move for the rest of the day.

"Where do you need to go?" he asked nervously.

"To Nile," Dummie said. He looked at the sun. "I know. Is end of afternoon. If sun is there at end of afternoon, Nile is other way," he said.

"And how do you steer this thing?"

Dummie pulled at the rope around its neck. "I think like this. Ghup ghup!"

For whatever reason, the dromedary seemed to agree with them and began to lumber in the right direction. The stubborn donkey suddenly trotted along after them obediently.

Angus dug his feet into the dromedary's back. They were going much too slowly. They must as well be on foot!

Then the animal began to bellow and broke into a trot.

Angus held on tight and looked back from time to

time. Soon the rocks were far behind them. The dromedary was enjoying it and headed in an easterly direction
at a fast trot. After a while, Angus saw the outline of the
step pyramid in the distance.

"We're going the right way!" he cried in relief. He
looked back and there was still no sign of anyone coming after them.

Just as suddenly as the dromedary had broken into a
trot, it seemed to tire of running. It took a couple more
steps, stood still and then began to chomp on a clump
of thorny bushes.

"Hey, stop that. Walk on!" Angus cried. They both
kicked the dromedary's sides but it was as if the animal
didn't even feel it. "We'll walk the last bit then," Angus
quickly decided. He looked back again and his heart
missed a beat. There was a cloud of dust in the desert
heading their way.

The step pyramid wasn't too far away, but the dust
cloud was approaching fast. "He'll have to come with
us, otherwise he'll give us away!" cried Angus. He
grabbed the dromedary's rope and they began to run.
"We'll never make it," he panted.

He looked back again and got a fright. The two
shapes riding the dromedary were clearly recognizable.
"We'll have to hide. There! That's your dad's spot again.
We'll go into that cave!"

They hastily pulled the dromedary to an overhanging
rock and pulled on its head until it sank through its
knees and lay down. Dummie pulled the donkey towards the entrance, pushed it through the cave's opening and tied its rope around the block in the middle.

They quickly crawled into the small recess at the back. Now all they could do was hope that the men hadn't seen them. They waited, their hearts pounding.

A while later they heard voices and footsteps.

"They'll see our tracks in the sand," Angus whispered. He pressed himself even further into the recess.

"Where's that dromedary?" Ted asked.

Immediately there was the gurgling sound of a dromedary inflating its throat.

"There," Angus said dejectedly.

"Here!" Harry cried triumphantly. "But where's the boy?"

"He must have continued on foot. It's not that much further," came Ted's voice. "Pity, boss. We've lost him."

"Hee-haw, hee-haw," the donkey said.

"Blasting cackdingle. Can't those stupid animals keep their mouths shut?" Angus whispered.

"Donkey is not stupid," Dummie said.

"No, but he is going to give us away!"

"Hee-haw! Hee-haw!"

There was the sound of running footsteps. "What's this? There's a donkey here! Tied up. Do you know what that means?" said Harry's voice, close by.

"Yes. No. I think..."

"That he's here, you fool. Must be. But how did he get a donkey?"

Angus made himself as small as possible. If the men

stuck their head around the corner, they still wouldn't see him. The sound of heavy breathing grew closer. Angus held his breath. "Not here, boss," Ted's voice said, near to his head. The breathing moved away again. Angus cautiously breathed out again.

"He can't have gone," Harry snapped. "He's hidden. Maybe there's another passageway here somewhere."

Angus saw movement out of the corner of his eye. He broke into a sweat. He stared wide-eyed at an enormous scorpion scuttling along a ledge towards his face. He moved his head as far as he could out of the way and tried not to breathe. The creature approached slowly, its tail raised.

"I see something!" Dummie hissed, suddenly excited.

"Me too!" squeaked Angus.

He heard Dummie move.

"Dummie, what do you do if... Is it dangerous?" The scorpion was now just a couple of centimetres away from him. "Help! Dummie!"

"Baff!" There was a loud crash as Dummie used a stone to reach over him and kill the scorpion.

"What was that?" The beam of a torch shone right into Angus' eyes. "There! He's there! Come here, you!" A hand roughly grabbed Angus by the arm and pulled him from the crack.

"How?!" Harry looked at the chain around his waist in disbelief. "How on earth did you manage to break that?"

"The... the ch-chain was b-broken... And I f-found a donkey outside," Angus stuttered.

"A donkey? Well, that's a strange coincidence. Did you also find a mobile phone by any chance?"

"Boss, he can't have telephoned for a donkey," Ted said foolishly.

"Shut up. Of course he's got his own phone. A millionaire's son. How stupid of us not to have checked. He must have called for help. Someone cut him loose. And he's hiding here too."

"Well, we'd better leave then. It might be a policeman," Ted said nervously.

"Policemen don't hide. No, it's that other boy. The burned one."

"But he'll call the police then, won't he?" Ted said.

"Do you see any police here?"

"No."

"Then shut up!"

Ted shut up, insulted.

"It's not true," Angus said quickly. "It wasn't the burned boy."

"Who then?"

"Nobody. I don't have a phone, look," Angus said.

"I don't believe you. You and I are going to have a little chat," Harry said threateningly.

"B-boss, b-b-boss!" Ted suddenly stammered.

Angus looked. Ted's eyes were almost bursting out of their sockets. He staggered backwards and stared fearfully past Harry's head. "I... I can see something! I can see... a mummy!"

"Just shut up for once, pal!" Harry snapped.

"Boss! It's behind you! Whaah! A monster! Eek!"

Harry spun around. The grip of his hands weakened and Angus pulled himself free. He stared at Dummie, aghast. Dummie had got undressed again and was standing at the entrance, his arms spread. Angus had already seen him naked, but it still shocked him. Those glowing eyes, the hole of his nose, those ragged bits of bandage and his skinny arms and legs... Dummie looked absolutely terrifying.

The men stood there, frozen with fear.

Dummie took a few steps towards them, held his arms in the air and opened his mouth wide. Then he let out a hideous roar that echoed off the cave walls at least ten times. Angus shuddered. Was this his friend?

Dummie picked up a rock from the ground and jumped forward with a new roar.

Then there was a crazy chase. It happened so fast, Angus could hardly follow it.

Harry recoiled, grabbed the donkey and stood behind it. Dummie jumped onto the donkey and Harry ducked away. Ted climbed onto the block and Dummie jumped after him and punched him off it. Harry raced to the exit but there was Dummie again. Harry and Ted ran for their lives with Dummie chasing them. They stumbled, fell, ducked away and scrambled to their feet again. Whimpering, the men tried to escape Dummie. But he was everywhere.

Angus' mind raced. He didn't understand what was happening. Why was Dummie doing this? They'd never be able to overpower those two men. And only one of them had to escape before the whole world knew that a living mummy existed. What was Dummie doing?

By now the donkey was in a panic. It kicked with all its legs at the same time and pulled hysterically at the rope attached to the block. Suddenly everything went wrong. Dummie ran behind the back of the donkey. The donkey bucked and its legs smacked hard into Dummie's stomach. Dummie flew through the air and landed on top of Ted. He screamed as though he was being skinned alive. As quick as a flash, Harry picked up a sharp stone and ran over to them.

"Dummie!" Angus yelled in horror.

At that same moment, Harry whacked Dummie on the head. Dummie screamed and fell backwards. With a triumphant cry, Harry jumped onto the donkey and kicked its sides. "Pull on that rope, Ted!" he shouted. "Pull the animal free!"

The donkey bucked and tensed its muscles.

Suddenly there was an ominous rumbling sound.

The block the donkey was tied to, was moving slowly. The donkey pulled harder and then everything happened all at once. The block toppled onto one side and the rope broke free. A deep hole was revealed. The edges of the hole crumbled away and it rapidly grew in size. A horrible roaring came from under the ground.

"Get out of here! The whole lot's collapsing!" shouted Harry. He let himself fall off the donkey, which then jumped away. At the same moment, the large block fell into the hole. Angus grabbed hold of the rope and pulled the donkey towards him with all his might. A moment later there was a thundering sound and half of the floor collapsed. The two men disappeared into the depths with a hideous scream.

Angus was frightened out of his skin. As an avalanche of dust and stones rained down on him, he pressed himself against the back wall of the cave. When the dust had settled, he found himself staring at an empty space in front of him. There now was a gaping hole where the floor had been. Angus' heart pounded in his chest. Where was Dummie? He cautiously went over to the edge of the hole. He could vaguely make out wooden poles at the sides. It looked like a trap. A trap?! Who on earth would build a trap in an abandoned cave? Somewhere deep below him came a terrified shriek.

"Dummie, is that you? Where are you?" Angus called anxiously.

To his horror, the sound started again. He dived back and held tight onto the donkey. And then something much worse happened. With a thunderous roar, the

whole entrance of the cave collapsed. Pieces of rock
hurtled down around him and a large piece grazed his
arm.

Then it was pitch black.

CHAPTER 8

The Tomb Of Akhnetut

"Dummie? Dummie!"

Angus held his arms out in front of him like a blind man. He slid his foot forward and took a cautious step. And another. And then he didn't dare go any further. Where was that hole? Had Dummie fallen down it too? "Dummie! Dummie! Help!"

Two golden eyes appeared next to him from nowhere and Angus screamed.

"I am ghere," whispered Dummie's voice. "Stay there!"

"What happened?"

"Men fall in ghole," Dummie said.

"But the entrance!"

"Entrance broken."

"Completely? Then we can't get out! Hey, what are you doing?"

"Don't move," Dummie ordered.

The golden eyes turned away and Angus heard something slide and a zip opening. All of a sudden a torch clicked on. Angus could just make out Dummie rummaging in a rucksack.

"Ghere is one more." Dummie returned and handed Angus a second torch.

Angus hurriedly turned it on. He held his breath. Right before his feet was an enormous hole. It was a miracle he hadn't fallen into it himself. He could hear Harry and Ted calling for help from its depths.

There was more space on the other side of the pit. They cautiously pulled the donkey to the other side. Only then did Angus shine his torch on the pile of rubble in front of the entrance. It was gigantic. Blocks as large as cows were piled up to the ceiling. Angus shuddered. The horrible reality hit him. The cave had completely collapsed and they were trapped. And no one knew they were here. He looked at Dummie in despair.

"We have to get out of here. We have to dig. We have to do something! Why did you have to take your clothes off? All that silly nonsense made the cave collapse. That's how it started. It's your fault! And now the men have seen you too! What did you do that?"

"Ghad to," Dummie said. He didn't sound frightened, more like cheerful.

"But why? Dummie, they know you're a mummy

now! Do you know what that means?"

"Means nothing," Dummie said. "They are in ghole. I ghave seen something. They ghad to gho. They could not see." Then he even began to laugh.

Angus didn't understand any of it. "Yes, but that pit... it was there deliberately. It's a kind of trap!"

"Yes. There is passage," Dummie said. And then he shone his torch on a black opening a metre above the ground, exactly on the spot they had hidden and seen the scorpion. A passage was now visible there and under it a ledge. Angus held his breath. The passage was square-shaped. Much too square-shaped.... It was manmade!

"What is that?" he whispered in disbelief.

"It is entrance," Dummie grinned.

"Entrance? What to? Oh, no... Is that...?" Angus clamped his mouth shut. A secret passageway near a burial ground in Egypt... this could only mean one thing! "Dummie, what did you see when I saw that scorpion? You said: I see something!"

"I saw this," Dummie said triumphantly. He shone his torch on a spot at the top right of the square hole. There was an oval shape with a few hieroglyphics carved into it. Angus held his breath. "Akhnetut's cartouche," he whispered.

"MAASHI. This is entrance to ghrave of my father," Dummie said. "You gho too?"

Angus sunk to the floor, overwhelmed. Here they were, trapped in a cave in the desert with a donkey and two kidnappers who'd fallen down a hole. And maybe they'd found the entrance to Akhnetut's grave. It was exactly what they'd been looking for. But... what did that matter now? They had to escape. What was the point of a grave if you couldn't get out of it?

Dummie grabbed hold of the ledge and pulled himself up.

"Coming?" he asked.

"Coming? No, of course not! I want to get out of here! And you! Put something on! There are bits of skin hanging off all over the place! Dummie, we have to get out of here! Blasting cackdingle! Get dressed!"

"No," said Dummie defiantly.

Angus' thoughts raced. Maybe the men had a phone. "Hang on," he cried. He picked up one of the rucksacks and looked inside. No phone. Just two extra torches, bread and water. And the other rucksack contained only bread and water.

"Come on!" Dummie called impatiently from the opening.

Angus hesitated and then threw one rucksack into the gaping hole in the floor. "HELP! Help us!" came the immediate reply.

"Sirᴂʀ! Whut urc you doing? You ghivc fuud?" Dummie cried angrily.

"Yes."

"But they arc cnemy!'

"Yes but otherwise they'll die!"

Dummie shrugged, turned around and climbed into the tunnel.

"Dummie! Do you think there's another entrance to that grave?" Angus said fearfully. "Dummie! We're trapped! Dummie! Come back!"

Dummie didn't reply. At his wits' end, Angus grabbed Dummie's clothes and the rope and climbed onto the ledge. On a sudden impulse, he got back down and tied the donkey tightly to a rock. "Stay. Don't move, or you'll fall in. I'll be back soon," he whispered. He patted its neck, climbed back up onto the ledge and crawled into the passageway.

Dummie was no longer to be seen.

"Dummie!" Angus shone his torch. The walls were rough and undecorated. There was a bend in the tunnel and then it sloped downwards. Angus crawled further, foot by foot. His heart was beating fast. What if everything collapsed? What if he got stuck now? Maybe it was a dead end. Or there was another trap. Were there scorpions here? Or those deaf snakes with the wide heads? What if his torch battery ran out? Was there enough air? Maybe they'd suffocate. They'd never get out of here! He pushed the thoughts away. There might be another exit in Akhnetut's grave. Otherwise... He paused for a moment and listened. There was a thud in the distance. And then a cry of joy. "Ghere! Ghere it is!"

He hurried on. The tunnel seemed endless. He felt his trousers tearing and his knees becoming scraped. He tried not to think of what might or might not be left of Dummie's knees. Maybe he was crawling over bits of Dummie's skin.

A few feet further, the passage suddenly became steeper. Angus slid down the last part and thudded clumsily onto a smooth floor. He quickly shone his torch around. He was in a long, empty room. And on the other side... His mouth gaped. On the other side, Dummie was standing in front of a massive golden door with large statues of people with animal heads on either side of it.

Angus got to his feet, hardly believing his eyes. He staggered over to it. His heart was pounding. A golden door, it had to lead to a grave. There was a seal on the door with Akhnetut's cartouche on it. And the seal was

still intact... Angus breathlessly stroked the round piece of resin.

"This is it," Dummie smiled.

"Yes. What now?" Angus stared at the large stone post holding the door shut. They'd never be able to lift it.

Dummie began to heave at it. "Ghelp me then."

"Help you?" Angus got crosser. "Wait a minute. All you think about is that grave! We're locked up in here!"

"Yes. You must ghelp. Do it!"

Angus hesitated. Then he angrily clamped the torch between his teeth and pushed along. The post didn't move an inch. "With shoulder. Push!" Angus closed his eyes, put his shoulders under the post and pushed with all his might. He was expecting Dummie to lose an arm at any minute. Or maybe even his head.

"Ghe ghoes!" cried Dummie. At the same moment, Angus felt the post move upwards. "Gharder. Push! No!" With a thud, the post sank back down.

"It'll never work. It's much too heavy," Angus panted.

"SIRSAR! Ghe must!" snapped Dummie. They tried again but the stone post was simply too heavy.

"Dummie, we can't do it. I want to go back. We have to get out. I—"

"Donkey must ghelp," said Dummie.

"What?" Angus looked at his grinning face in astonishment.

"Donkey is strong. Must ghelp."

"Have you lost your mind? You don't want to fetch the donkey? And get it through that passage? It'll never fit!"

"Donkey must. I gho ghet ghim."

Before Angus could stop him, Dummie had crawled back into the tunnel. "You've gone stark raving mad!" Angus shouted. He looked at the two gods on either side of the door. It was as though their black eyes were staring straight through him. Angus shuddered, ran back to the hole and hurried after Dummie.

Dummie had already untied the donkey and was standing in front of the hole. The animal was braying pitifully and from deep in the pit came the cries for help from the men. Angus automatically shone his torch on the pile of rubble blocking the entrance. They were never going to get out that way.

"Angus, take donkey!" Dummie ordered.

"What do you mean? How's he going to get in there?" Angus said in a panic.

"You gho first. I push ghim," Dummie said.

Angus shook his head in disbelief, but Dummie had already begun to push. Angus took the rope and pulled the donkey's head upwards. At the same time, Dummie slapped its rear. It was unbelievable but the donkey brayed and put its front legs into the passage. Dummie gave the donkey another whack. The donkey kicked its back legs, scrambled up and a moment later was wedged tightly in the passage on its knees. Angus was at a loss. What now? The donkey blocked the entire space! The only way he could go was back to the grave.

And what about the passageway? It could collapse any minute. Blasting cackdingle, they were never going to get out!

The donkey brayed and Angus began to pull. Slowly the donkey edged its way, bit by bit. Further along, the passage was a bit wider and the donkey would have more space to breathe. But they couldn't go any faster. Inch by inch, they wrestled the donkey through the tunnel. Angus was boiling hot. To make matters worse, his torch began to flicker. He hit it against the ground and it came on again.

After what seemed like an eternity, they reached the steep slope. Angus slid down, ducked to one side and the confused donkey thudded to the floor beside him.

Angus lay on the ground in exhaustion. Sweat was

running from his hair in streams, all his muscles hurt and his heart was beating like a drum.

Dummie seemed tireless. He fell on top of the donkey, jumped off, grabbed the rope that Angus had brought along with the clothes and went to the door. "Rope ghoes around ghere," he said. He wriggled and pulled until he'd got the rope through the chink between the stone post and the door. Then he tied a big knot in it, took the other end to the donkey and tied it around its neck. Angus was still on the ground. He felt like crying. Dummie had gone totally mad. If only he'd just stayed with the men in the cave. Then Mr Greystone would have paid the ransom money and he wouldn't be trapped here now. This was ten times worse. A thousand times.

"You don't ghelp?" Dummie asked crossly.

Angus got up. "What do I need to do?" he asked, tired.

"Donkey must pull. You pull too."

"But that poor animal," Angus protested weakly.

"Donkey is not poor. Pulling is donkey's job. Come on."

Angus took the rope and Dummie stood next to the donkey.

"When I say ghup, you pull rope," Dummie said. His glowing eyes stared at Angus. "You do?"

"Yes, I do," Angus said meekly.

"MAASHI... Ghup!"

He gave the donkey a whack on its backside and Angus pulled.

Something creaked.

"Again! MAASHI... Ghup! Ghup!"

At the third pull, the post broke free and fell to the floor with a deafening crash. It had broken in two. Angus toppled backwards and the donkey brayed in fright.

"Ghooray! It worked!" screamed Dummie. He ran to the golden door, grabbed the handle and turned around. His entire face was grinning and his eyes were glowing so brightly that it was though he was on fire. Angus didn't know whether to laugh or cry.

"Angus. Come with me. You are my friend. We gho see. Now!"

And then he broke the seal and slowly opened the door.

Angus would never forget the sight that greeted him. A strong smell gushed from the silent darkness. It struck him that this was the way someone had once discovered the tomb of Tutankhamen. Angus shone his torch inside almost reverently. Then all of his thoughts disappeared. He didn't even think about being trapped anymore. He gazed open-mouthed at all the riches before them.

Akhnetut's burial chamber was small and packed from floor to ceiling with objects. Angus could see wooden vases, golden plates and containers, a bier, a small throne, a cupboard full of vases, a golden chair, large and small statues made of different types of wood.

There was a strong smell of perfume, oils and wood. There were rolled up carpets, jewellery, wreaths, things that looked like fruit and lots and lots more.

The donkey had stopped braying and the only sound Angus could hear was his own pounding heart.

Dummie cautiously walked past the treasure to the golden coffin in the middle. There were a gold sceptre and a whip on top of the coffin, and next to them, the double crown of Egypt. There was a hole in the middle of the first crown. Dummie's hand automatically reached for his scarab. Angus knew why: it was the hole where Dummie's scarab had been.

To the left of the coffin was a small golden altar with four jars on top. Dummie had told him about these. Three of them depicted animal heads and the fourth a human head. Angus shuddered. Akhnetut's brains were in one of the jars, maybe in the one with the monkey head on it.

Dummie closed his eyes. As he stood there without moving, Angus looked around the room, almost entranced. He felt weak in the knees. The smell. Maybe it was the strong smell. All that gold...

Dummie opened his eyes again. Just as entranced, he shone his torch on all the objects, and in particular over the walls. On hieroglyphics and pictures of gods, animals, a group of birds and people. Suddenly his torch swung back. The light rested on a group of birds.

"My drawing," he whispered. And then loudly, "MAASHI! Angus! There is my drawing!"

"What?" Angus came to his senses. In disbelief, he stared at the drawing of white birds with long elegant necks.

The bird in the middle had its wings spread and almost seemed to be dancing. "You can't have drawn that," he whispered.

"I did! That is my drawing for Sadihotep. This is wall of Sadihotep!" Dummie cried.

It was a while before it sunk in. The wall of Sadihotep? The wall of... Suddenly he shouted out in relief. "Dummie, so we must be in your grandad's pyramid! Remember you said the burial chamber was smaller! This room is behind it! They built a new wall! We're in Sadihotep's pyramid!"

Dummie grinned. "I was sure," he said.

"Do you know what that means?" Angus said in excitement. "We might be able to get out!"

"No. Means my dad is buried with own dad," Dummie said contentedly.

"Did they do that then?"

"I don't know. Maybe ghe knew ghe die, and they decided. Maybe Ghepsetsut. Dad loved Sadihotep."

They looked at each other. They'd never find out. But Akhnetut's grave would never be found either. Who would ever look for a grave in a grave?

"We'll have to go through this wall then," Angus said in agitation. He inspected the wall between them and Sadihotep's burial chamber. He had no idea how thick it was, but he couldn't see a single irregularity, let alone a door or anything.

"Do you know how they did it? I mean, how they closed off something like this?"

"Can't gho through wall," Dummie said dejectedly.

"No, no just like that, not without a drill. We've only

got our hands. But could there be a secret door or something? Like you press on a button and the wall turns?" No. Of course that was just in films.

He had another look at the wall, but couldn't see anything at all.

Angus' mind worked feverishly. "Then we'd better shout for help, so they can hear us. There are tourists in Sadihotep's grave every day. If we shout loudly enough they might hear us."

"Can't gho through wall," Dummie repeated.

"But we have to," said Angus.

"No," said Dummie.

Angus looked at Dummie, astonished. "Why not? It's our only chance."

"If you shout, I ghit you."

"What? What do you mean?"

"You don't shout! No one can know. Because otherwise they find ghrave of my father. Cannot."

Angus suddenly realized what Dummie meant. Dummie didn't want to find a way into Sadihotep's grave at all! He wanted to protect Akhnetut's grave!

"But then we'll die in here!" Angus cried out incredulously.

"Maybe. But ghrave must stay ghidden. My dad must travel with things. Wall cannot open!"

Angus took a step back. He looked at Dummie's stubborn face in disgust. He was his best friend and he wanted them to die here? He was furious.

"Are you crazy? You might not care, you're already dead. But I'm not! I don't want to die in this tomb! I want my dad. I want to go back to The Netherlands! I'm sick of stupid Egypt. Everything's old or broken or dead here. And I got kidnapped."

"I ghelp you escape!"

"Yes, and now I'm trapped again. Here, in a burial chamber! I want to go home! I'm on holiday! I want to go to the beach! I want to cycle past fields of cows! See grass! I've had enough of stupid, stupid Egypt!"

"My ghome is nicc!" snapped Dummie.

"Whatever. That doesn't help me!" Angus shouted furiously. "I'm going to stand next to your stupid birds and when I hear someone, I'm going to yell."

"No, you don't!"

"I will!"

"No!"

Shaking with fury, Angus stood face to face with Dummie. He balled his fists. "If I hadn't tied up the donkey, he would have fallen in the pit and we'd never have been able to use him! You're only here because of me!" he shouted, beside himself with rage. "I want to get out. My dad must be really worried!"

"And my dad must travel," Dummie said, just as angrily. He grabbed Angus' raised hand and held it tightly.

Angus exploded. "I don't care about your dad!" he screamed hysterically. "My dad's still alive at least! And I don't want to die! Let me go! You idiot!"

Dummie pushed his head against Angus'. They stood there for maybe ten seconds angrily staring at each other. Then Dummie cried, "SIRSAR!" He let Angus go, turned around and sat on the floor, leaning against the sarcophagus. Angus looked around. His eye fell on

the golden sceptre on top of the sarcophagus. Now he felt like whacking Dummie on the head with the sceptre. It frightened him. He'd never felt anything like this before. Could he hit his best friend? Was he really thinking this? Did he really want to? No...

His shoulders slumped. He ran his torch over the walls again with a suppressed sob. He stopped at the drawing of the birds. It was a lovely drawing made four thousand years ago by a little boy for his grandfather's grave. He pictured Dummie kneeling with pots of paint and brushes. Maybe he'd cried while he was painting. It was just awful.

And then Angus began to cry. He sunk to the floor and sobbed his heart out. His shoulders jerked. "I want my dad," he sobbed. "I don't want to die here. You are just a mean, mean, mean ratbag! I wish I'd never met you. I wish you'd gone into someone else's house. Or that we'd called the museum. Or the police. They'd have taken you away. I wish I'd never met you! Never." He cried with anger and sadness. For himself and for Dummie.

Suddenly he felt a skinny arm on his shoulder. He pushed the arm away, but it came back. Bony fingers awkwardly rubbed his back.

"Stop," Dummie whispered.

It only made Angus cry even more.

"Stop with crying! I don't mean like that," Dummie said gently. "You are big friend."

"I don't mean it like that either," sobbed Angus. "I'm glad we've found your dad. But now my I want my own dad."

Dummie sighed. Then he got up, picked up the pile of Ted's clothes and put on Ted's shirt. "Alright. We gho to Sadihotep," he said. "But you cannot scream. We gho ourself."

"Oh, forget it," Angus cried. "We'll never break down that wall."

"Maybe I know," Dummie said.

Angus looked up with tear-filled eyes at Dummie who was carefully feeling along every place of the wall with his ragged fingers. "What are you looking for?" he sniveled.

Dummie said nothing but continued. All of a sudden his hand stopped. "Ghere is it. Secret door," he said quietly.

"A secret door?" Angus suddenly felt his courage

return. He got up. Everything ached and he felt awful.

"C-can you open it?" he stuttered.

"I think so," Dummie said. He carried on searching with his hands. "Ghere!"

Angus stared at a few tiny notches in the wall. Then he saw thin lines that formed a rectangle on the wall. "Is that the door?"

Dummie pushed his dried-up fingernails into the cracks, scratched away a bit of cement and began to push. To Angus' surprise, part of the wall slid back in its entirety. The secret door was simply a rectangular block, completely smooth and carved to fit perfectly.

"Wait a minute. What time is it?" Angus suddenly asked. They thought for a moment. It must be late in the evening, maybe even nighttime.

"Alright, we can do it then." Angus kneeled and began to push too. The block moved back, inch by inch, with a grating sound. After a while, a crack appeared beside it, and then a hole. Soon Angus could stick his whole hand through it. Just a bit more and then they'd be out. He almost felt like whooping with joy.

"Not fast. Don't break it," said Dummie.

They pushed until they could fit through the opening. Angus crawled through it first. He took a deep breath. An indescribable sense of relief flowed through him. They were free. He'd see his dad again. He wasn't going to die.

He looked around. The door was exactly behind Sadihotep's stone sarcophagus.

"Dummie? Where have you gone?"

"Ghere!" The donkey's head poked through the hole. Dummie had tied its mouth shut with the rope and the animal was snorting in fear. Angus pushed the door open wider and pulled the donkey into the burial chamber. He could just fit behind the sarcophagus. Angus carefully pushed him into the middle of the room.

Dummie was still in the tomb. Angus shone his lamp through the hole and saw Dummie standing next to his father's coffin. He was holding the scarab and muttering something incomprehensible. Angus quickly turned around. Dummie was saying goodbye to his dad. He mustn't disturb him. He walked back to the donkey and stroked its head. "You're the only donkey who has ever been in a pharaoh's grave," he whispered into its ear. "And remember not to tell anybody."
He bit his lip. If he told anyone about this, they'd be rich. They even become famous, they'd be on TV all over the world because they'd found an undisturbed grave with everything still in it. "Dutch boy finds pharaoh's tomb." He shook his head. No, he'd never do that.

All of a sudden there was a flash of light from the burial chamber. And then another, and another. Angus almost jumped out of his skin. "What's happening, Dummie?"

"Nothing. I make photo," Dummie called.

Angus almost burst out laughing from the nerves.

At last Dummie crawled out into Sadihotep's burial chamber. He was carrying Ted's rolled up trousers and the rope.

"Come on. Door must gho back," he said. They

kneeled on the floor and carefully pushed the block back into the hole. Angus shone his torch over the notches. Black stripes had been painted onto them, next to columns of hieroglyphics, as though they belonged there. Even if you looked really attentively, you'd think there was just a crack in the wall. It was no wonder nobody had ever discovered the secret door.

Angus and Dummie used their hands to smooth over the sand and shone their torches on the door and the ground again. There was no trace. No one would ever find this.

They got up.

"And now for the donkey," Angus said. "That poor creature has to get through another tunnel."

"This tunnel is bigger," Dummie said.

Well, yes, that was true.

"I gho check nobody is there." Dummie went into the gallery and disappeared. After a few minutes he returned. "I see no one," he said.

"Not any guards?"

"There is man. At tomb opposite. But I think ghe is sleeping."

"Alright. Hang on." Angus took off his T-shirt and tore it into four strips. As Dummie stared in amazement, Angus used the rope to tie the strips around the donkey's hooves. "He'll be quieter if he's wearing socks," he explained. "Right, let's go."

They pushed the donkey through the gap in the entrance room and then into the passageway. This passage was indeed bigger and it was easier for the donkey to get along it. It did shake its head wildly but it couldn't bray, only snort. Its nostrils constantly opened and shut. "Keep going," Angus said gently. "We're almost there." And there were the steep steps. Angus looked up and saw a black hole with white dots. The sky. He'd never been so happy to see the stars before. He climbed the steps and stuck his head out of the hole.

Further along on the other side of the track, in front of another tomb, there was indeed a man on a chair. But even from here, his snoring was audible. "Alright, come on," he called quietly. Using all the strength they had left, they pushed and pulled the donkey up the steps. Finally they were outside.

"Over there," Angus pointed. Without making a sound, they walked around the pyramid until they were out of sight of the sleeping man. There was no cry, no scream, nothing at all. Angus exhaled in relief and then his knees almost gave way. They'd managed it, they were out. But now what? "Let's find a safe place to spend the night first," he whispered. "Over there, near your father's rocks. I want to see what it looks like.'

They quietly walked on. Angus thought about the narrow tunnel he'd crawled along right under their feet and shuddered. When they reached the rocks, they walked around to the cave entrance. There was nothing left of it. Everything had collapsed and no one could tell that there was a cave hidden behind it.

Angus pressed his head to the stones and listened carefully. Very far in the distance were faint cries for help.

"I can hear the men," he said, no longer afraid. "We have to free them."

"No. They are enemy. Leave them there."

"But then they'll die!"

"So what. They will be mummies," Dummie said.

"No! I don't want that!" cried Angus.

"If this ghole opens, everyone see entrance to ghrave. Cannot," Dummie said.

Angus looked at the stubborn face in dismay. Naturally he understood that Dummie wanted his father to journey on without being disturbed. But you couldn't just let two men die because another person was already dead.

"Dummie, that's not right. Then you'd be a murderer."

"They are enemy."

"But I don't want it!"

"I do," said Dummie. "They ghave seen me. They tell about mummy. Cannot."

"Oh yes, that too... But no one will believe them, will they?"

"Maybe."

Angus closed his eyes. A wave of exhaustion washed over him. He shivered. It was cold. And they weren't out of danger yet. How were they going to get back to Cairo? On foot? It was much too far. He didn't even know the way. They had to wait until it got light and then try to arrange something. And Dummie had to put on some clothes. He could still put on Ted's trousers but then his face and hands were still bare. Even the biggest ass would see that Dummie was a mummy. Angus shook his head. "We'll stay here until it gets light," he decided, tiredly. "Let's rest against the donkey." They pulled the donkey down and Angus cuddled up to it. Dummie stopped talking and so did he. He was totally knackered. He closed his eyes and thought about everything they had been through. His head spun. He couldn't believe it all himself. No one would ever believe this story.

Dummie woke him up. "Sun coming from Nut soon," he said. "Sun comes fast."

Angus blinked and found himself staring right into the donkey's face. He was wide awake at once. He stood up and saw the sky growing lighter at the horizon. Light. Morning. They'd escaped and they had to get out of here. But how? His thoughts raced again. New groups of tourists would arrive in the morning. If they went to the carpark, they might be able to take an early taxi back. But then Dummie would need some clothes.

"Dummie, I've got an idea. You wear my trousers. Then we'll rip up Ted's trousers and bind them around your head and hands. Then we'll get a taxi and we'll go to the hotel," he said. "Dad will know what to do. And so will Mr Greystone."

Dummie shook his head. "No," he said.

"No? But you can't come like that."

Dummie turned his head to the desert. And then I said something terrible. "I don't gho to ghotel."

"What?" It was as though Angus had been slapped across the face.

"You gho to ghotel," Dummie said. "I stay ghere."

"Here?" Angus cried, his voice cracking. "Why? What are you going to do?"

"Because I want. I must.'

Angus fearfully grabbed his hand. "Dummie, you have to come with me," he pleaded. "I won't leave you here on your own. I— Dummie, you're my friend!"

"I know. But I stay ghere. You gho to ghotel and tell no one."

"About what? The grave? I can tell Nick, can't it?"

"Nick is not no one. But Mr Greystone must not know. No one."

Angus started to feel desperate. "Of course I won't tell. But... Dummie, at least put some clothes on. You'll need them when you come back later. Dummie?"

"I do not need," Dummie said.

"But you can't go back like that!" Angus stared at Dummie in bewilderment.

Dummie unwrapped the rope from around the nose's nose. He picked up Ted's rolled up trousers and climbed onto its back. "You gho to ghotel?" he said.

Angus suddenly felt afraid. Very afraid. He looked at his friend in the much too baggy shirt with just a few ragged bits of left-over bandage around his dried-up body, a camera and a golden scarab. His friend who was sitting on a donkey and sending him away.

"Dummie... will I see you again? Please?"

Dummie stared into the distance. Then he turned back. "Yes. You see me." Then he kicked his black feet against the donkey's sides and trotted off. He disappeared into the desert in a cloud of dust.

Angus watched him until he could no longer see him. Then he turned around despondently and looked at the sky. It was quickly getting light. His stomach was hurting, he was so hunger, and he was thirsty too.

He began to walk wearily. He trudged over the hills to the big step pyramid, and walked along the arcade to the carpark. There weren't any tourists yet, but he didn't even look for them. He didn't just have a stone in his belly but a massive block of rock. A couple of people selling things waved to him from where they were

sitting. Two men came over to him and started excitedly
shouting things he couldn't understand. "Cʜᴏᴋʀᴀɴ,"
he muttered.

One of the men picked up a scarf and wrapped it
around his neck. He gestured that Angus could keep it.

"Thank you." Angus murmured. They gave him water
and because he didn't say anything else, they left him
alone. He sat down on a wall. His head was spinning
again. Akhnetut's grave was full of gold. Those two men
were stuck in a pit. And Dummie. He should never
have left Dummie alone. What had Mr Scribble said to

him? "Whatever happens, bring him back with you."
And now he'd left Dummie behind in the desert. Without any proper clothing or shoes. But it had been impossible to stop him. What would his dad say? His dad... all he wanted now was to see his dad.

After a while, the first bus drove into the carpark. And right after that a couple of taxis appeared. Angus got up and walked over to one. He knew he looked terrible wearing dusty torn trousers and a brand new scarf.

He felt in his pocket for the hotel's card and gave it to the taxi driver who began to chatter away. Angus got the money his father had given him out of his pocket and the man talked even faster. But because Angus didn't reply, the driver finally just got in and started the engine. Soon they were driving along the road past the green fields and later through the bumper-car traffic of Cairo. Angus looked out of the window but didn't take anything in. He snoozed and then fell asleep.

Finally they stopped in front of the hotel. Angus paid and went to the entrance.

A guard in a blue uniform blocked his way. But before he could say anything Angus spotted his father in the lobby. "Dad! Dad!" he cried.

"Angus," his father shouted at the same instant.

Angus pushed the guard out of the way, flew into his father's arms and held him tight like he never wanted to let him go. Then he burst into tears. Nick held him just as tightly, then held him at arm's length to look at him, and then hugged him again.

"Angus, son, what happened? What did they do to you? I've been so worried."

"It was those men from the hotel, in a cave," Angus sobbed. "They've seen Dummie. Dad, we found the grave!"

"What?"

"Akhnetut's grave! But Dummie has gone. I... I don't know."

A couple of people looked over at them with curiosity and Nick pulled Angus toward the lifts. They walked down the corridor to their room and Nick locked the door behind them. He sat down on the bed and pulled Angus onto his lap. "Start at the beginning," he said gently.

Angus took a deep breath and began to tell him about the cave at the place where they looked for Akhnetut's grave and didn't find it. About the kidnapping, about being tied up in another cave, about the escape with the dromedary and the donkey, and then the first cave again, how Dummie had got undressed and scared everybody. About the hole in the ground and the collapsed entrance, about the secret tunnel and finally about Akhnetut's tomb.

"We pushed the donkey through the tunnel. It helped us open the door. And then we were in the grave. Dad, it was... out of this world. It was packed full. And the jars with the brains in it were there. And all those things, like in the museum. And Dad, Dummie was right about the drawing. The drawing of the birds was there too! And when we saw it, we knew we must be in Sadihotep's pyramid. And then we went through the wall and then..." Angus began to cry again. "... then Dummie wanted to stay there—"

"Whumpy dumpman," whispered Nick. He pulled Angus closer.

"We had a horrible argument, Dad. I almost hit him. He wanted to stay in that grave with me—"

"And where's Dummie now?" his father asked.

"I don't know," Angus sobbed. "Somewhere on that donkey in the desert. Without proper clothes." He looked up and saw the bags under his father's eyes. "Are you better now or not?"

"I feel much better now that you've come back," Nick said. But his voice sounded as though he was about to cry. They sat together for a while.

"That chain—" Angus said.

"Which chain?"

Angus lifted up his scarf.

"Poor boy." Nick stood up in alarm, got a paperclip and fiddled with it until he got the lock to spring open. The chain fell to the ground and Nick put it in a suitcase. "We need to go Mr Greystone," he said in tired voice. "We have to tell him everything."

"Yes. No. Wait. We can't tell him everything. Those kidnappers—"

"They're still trapped down a hole, aren't they? We'll call the police so they can go and arrest them."

"No, we can't."

"Why not? They can just dig through the rubble. Egyptians are very good at digging."

"Don't you get it?" Angus said unhappily. "If they open the cave, they'll find the entrance to Akhnetut's tomb. Dummie doesn't want that. He thinks the men should just die in there."

"Well, I don't think so," said Nick. "I don't want that on my conscience."

"Me neither," Angus whispered. "But I don't want anyone to find Akhnetut's grave either. And you don't want that, do you, Dad?"

Nick scratched his chin and thought hard.

"What should we do?" Angus asked quietly.

"Free those two," Nick said. "And then look for Dummie. The two of us. Listen. I have an idea. We'll do it like this..."

Ten minutes later, Nick and Angus knocked on Mr Greystone's door.

Mr Greystone opened up. He hadn't shaved and he was holding a telephone. He was very startled. "Angus? Angus? Angus!"

He took a step forward and almost flattened Angus to his fat belly. "Soapy sludgeball! It's really you! Did they let you go?"

"He escaped," Nick said. "Dummie helped him get away."

"Is that true? Unbelievable. Amazing! No, how awful. What happened? And where's Dummie?"

"Upstairs in bed," Nick said. "He's completely exhausted. Let him sleep. Is Dimitri still with that teacher?"

"Yes. Good heavens, Angus. Tell me everything!"

The three of them sat down on Mr Greystone's bed and Angus told the entire story again. But now he stopped after escaping on the dromedary with the donkey. "And then I was free again. Thanks to Dummie," he finished.

"Soapy sludgeball," Mr Greystone said again.

"Did you call the police?" Angus asked.

"When I lost the two of you, I did. But then the men called about the kidnapping and I told the police you'd come back. And I had Dimitri go and stay with one of the teachers from his school. He doesn't know about anything, he thinks I had to work. Angus, the kidnapper was threatening to harm you. Did they hurt you?"

"No," Angus said. "They just gave me food and drink."

Mr Greystone rubbed his forehead. "Well, you escaped just in time," he said. "I was going to pay the ransom money this afternoon."

"A million? For someone else's kid?"

"If it hadn't been you, Dimitri would have been kidnapped," Mr Greystone said simply. "In fact I should be grateful to you. And Dummie in particular. When can I talk to him?"

"Not now, in any case. Later, I expect," Nick said vaguely.

Mr Greystone got up. "Then I'm going to call the police. They might still be able to find some clues. Would you still recognize the place, Angus?"

"No, it was somewhere in the desert," Angus lied.

"And those kidnappers? Did you get a good luck at them? Do you have a description?"

"No. I never saw them. And I didn't see their faces either, they were wearing masks. They went off into the desert on a camel."

Mr Greystone went over to the window and began to rock back and forth on his feet. He rubbed his bald head indecisively. "So it doesn't really make much sense to call the police," he said, reluctantly.

Nick nodded. "It'll probably only cause a lot of bother," he said.

"Well, I don't mind that. On the other hand, I do want to go home with Dimitri as soon as I can."

Nick nodded understandingly.

"Alright. Then we'll skip the police. I'm going to pick up Dimitri from that teacher's house and then we'll meet up again in the afternoon. Alright?"

Nick nodded for the third time.

"Alright, we have a plan." Mr Greystone hugged Angus again and went to the door. Angus grabbed his hand. "Thank you for not telling them I wasn't Dimitri," he said.

"Well of course I wouldn't do that. It's no skin off my pig nose. It might even have been my fault. I gave you Dimitri's cap."

"Oh. I'm afraid I've lost it," Angus said.

Mr Greystone burst out laughing. "That's what I was worried about the most, that cap," he said. "I'm off to get Dimitri. See you later."

CHAPTER 9

A Souvenir

Angus and his father hurried back to their room. Nick insisted that Angus stand under the shower for a minute first. Then he quickly put on some clean clothes and got his straw hat. Then they went downstairs and took a taxi to Sakkara. The piece of rock in his belly was still there. He had let Dummie go. Dummie had gone. And it was his fault.

The man who had given him the scarf, waved and smiled. Angus waved back and hurried after his father. They walked straight into the desert to Sadihotep's pyramid. "So it's over there," Angus pointed. They walked around the pyramid to the rocky outcrop, Angus leading the way.

"It's at the back. Here. It's here." Nick stared in dismay at the amount of rubble lying in front of them. "They're behind this lot? Whumpy dumpman. We'll never manage it."

Angus shuddered. More had collapsed in the meantime and the pile was even bigger than that morning. He pressed his ear to the rocks and listened, concerned. "I can't hear them anymore," he said. And then fearfully, "I can't help it. I did give them water, Dad. And food. They have to be alive. They have to!"

"Let me listen," Nick said. He pressed his head to the stones.

"Men not dead," a voice said at the same moment.

Angus spun around. Dummie stepped out from behind a rock. He was almost entirely naked. There was practically nothing left of Ted's shirt. Bits of skin hung off all over the place and he looked simply dreadful.

"Dummie!" Nick cried. He stared in shock at Dummie's bare face, arms and legs. "Whumpy, whumpy dumpman!'

"Dummie!" Angus rushed to him and almost squeezed him flat. "You're still here! You're back!"

Dummie freed himself. "Of course I am. I wait ghere for you."

"Wait for me? What do you mean?"

"I know you come back. But thieves are ghone," Dummie said. "I let them gho."

"What? You freed them? How did you do it?"

"With donkey," Dummie said proudly. "I went in cave, donkey pulled men up with rope."

"But how did you get in there?"

"Also with donkey," Dummie said. "Donkey made ghole. Donkey work very ghard."

Angus could hardly believe his ears. Dummie had released the two men? "But why? You said they were the enemy."

Dummie shrugged. "Otherwise you do it. I know you. You don't let men die. I knew you would come ghere. But I prefer to do it. I wait ghere for you."

Now Angus understood. That's why Dummie hadn't wanted to come with him this morning. He wanted to free the thieves first. He knew Angus would do it otherwise.

"I would never have told people about your dad's grave," he said quietly.

"I know. But maybe you come with Nick. Nick is not ghandy."

"What do you mean I'm not handy?" Nick said indignantly.

Dummie grinned. "Doesn't matter. Is all done now. I do it. I can do better than you. I am very ghood."

"Did those men see you again?" Angus asked.

Dummie's grin grew even bigger. He said he hadn't pulled them out of the pit until they'd been blindfolded. Harry came up first without a blindfold and Dummie had simply dropped him in again. The second time they'd both had blindfolds. He'd sent them off into the desert on the dromedary still wearing them.

"And did they just do what you said?"

"I shout loud. They are frightened to see mummy again. Very scared. They ghad argument," Dummie said.

"And where are they now?"

"That way somewhere. Someone will find." Dummie shrugged.

Well, Angus hoped so. He looked at the rubble in front of him. It resembled a pile of rocks like there were so many of around here. Dummie had smoothed out the sand in the area and there was no trace of anything strange having happened. Let alone that there was a grave here.

"Put my clothes on first," Angus said.

He took off his T-shirt and trousers and his shoes. Then they looked for something to put on Dummie's head.

"Ted's clothes?" Angus suggested.

"No, is all broken," Dummie said.

"My underpants then," said Nick. He took off his trousers, looked around, stepped out of his pants and put his trousers back on. He carefully tied his pants around Dummie's head.

"Well, just as well you don't have a nose anymore," giggled Angus. "My dad's pants!"

"It's a clean pair," Nick said indignantly. "And my pants never stink as badly as Dummie does!"

When Dummie was completely wrapped up, Nick gave Angus his long-sleeved shirt. It almost came down to Angus' knees. "What about you then?" Angus asked.

"I'll just go bare chested," Nick said.

Dummie gathered up Ted's rags and they walked back to Sadihotep's pyramid together. They looked like tramps, Angus thought to himself. Of the three of them, Dummie actually looked the most normal.

A group of tourists stared at them in astonishment.

"Boo!" Nick said and then hurried on in shock.

Angus spluttered.

When they arrived back at the pyramid, all three of them wanted to take another look inside. They went to the entrance and climbed down the steep staircase for the second time. Soon they were in the burial chamber.

"It was there, behind the coffin," Angus whispered. Nick inspected the length of the wall.

"You can't see, eh?" Dummie said.

"Oh but I can see something, something very bad!" Nick said. He bent down and picked something up.

"What?" Dummie asked in shock.

"This!" Nick held up a long strand of hair.

"Oh, that's from the donkey," Angus giggled in relief. "Where is the donkey now?"

"With other donkeys. I took back of course," Dummie said proudly.

Five minutes later they were back outside. It was getting hot again and Dummie began to smell more and more of dead mice. "Shall we just go then?" Nick asked. He wrapped his arms around Angus and Dummie and they strolled toward the step pyramid.

"Dummie, I want to tell you something," Nick said. "You have been fantastic."

"Yes, I am very ghood," Dummie said conceitedly.

Nick burst out laughing. "You are right. If it hadn't been for you..." He stopped talking and shook his head. "No, that's wrong. You're not fantastic. If it hadn't been for you, we wouldn't have been in Egypt."

"But without me you don't see my nice country," Dummie snorted.

"You mean this big sandpit?" Nick teased.

"With nice things. Is broken but very nice," Dummie laughed.

"Alright, you are fantastic," grinned Nick.

"Without me, no one know about Akhnetut," Dummie continued. "Without me, we are only in Polderdam. Without me, everything is boring!"

"Quiet and peaceful, you mean," Nick replied.

They turned left.

"Angus is ghood too. Without Angus, I don't have ghood friend," Dummie said.

"Yes, and now you're going to say that Mr Greystone is good," Nick said.

"Of course Mr Greystone is ghood," Dummie replied.

"Oh really? Without Mr Greystone, Angus wouldn't have been kidnapped."

"But because Angus kidnapped, I found ghrave."

Nick had to laugh again. "Alright. Then Mr Greystone is good too. And the donkey is good?"

"No, not donkey. Ghe betray us," Dummie said.

"But the floor collapsed because of the donkey," Angus said.

"Maashi. Then donkey is ghood. Everyone is ghood."

"And me?" Nick asked.

Dummie thought for a moment. "You ghad to poop lots. Also ghood," he giggled then.

"Yes," Nick said drily. "I was amazing at that."

The man with the scarves was standing in the carpark. He looked at Angus' bare legs and feet in astonishment. "He gave me a free scarf this morning, Dad," Angus said.

Nick went over to him, bought three scarves and gave the man a big tip.

"Nothing else! Chocolate! Chocolate!" he cried cheerfully.

Then they got into a taxi and drove off without looking back.

The porter at the hotel was just as astonished at their clothing. And when Dummie walked past him, he pulled a face and stuck his nose in the air. Nick smiled in a friendly way and hurried Dummie and Angus to the lifts.

Angus had another shower. As he was drying himself, he heard his father complaining.

"Stand still for once," Nick muttered.

"I stand still! You are not ghandy," Dummie said.

"I am handy. But you're waving your arms about."

"Because I am airplane!" Dummie cried.

"Shut up about flying!"

Angus peered around the corner from the bathroom and saw his father busying himself with new rolls of bandage. Dummie saw him, gave him a golden wink and did a pirouette, making Nick have to start all over again.

Angus burst out laughing. He was exhausted, but the squabbling was so funny.

When everyone was done, Angus sewed a new flap in front of Dummie's face. Finally they sprayed enough toilet freshener on Dummie to cover his own stench. Then they went to Mr Greystone's room.

Mr Greystone opened up cautiously. But as soon as he saw Dummie he threw open the door and hugged him. "Dummie!" he cried. "They told me everything. You're a hero. A real hero!"

"Are you leaving already?" Nick asked in surprise. He pointed at the two packed suitcases.

"Yes," Mr Greystone said. "I don't want to stay anymore. Dimitri's mother wants us to come back too. She's so worried. And I understand that." He stared ahead. "Only... there's something that's still bothering me," he said.

"You still want to call the police, don't you?" Nick said.

"Yes, I do. I'm not used to just letting things drop. But I won't. More unwelcome publicity about our family... And of course those men will have disappeared without trace. Try finding two men in Cairo."

"No, you'll never find them here," Angus muttered.

Mr Greystone shrugged. "You know, I've got Dimitri, and I've still got the money. We're just going to go home."

Nick smiled. "You could still try, you know. Nothing ventured, nothing gained. You never know, we might find them and we could throw them into a hole in the ground so they'd become mummies."

"Dad, if he doesn't want to," Angus said.

"Huh?"

"Sausage roll!" Angus said. "But not now!"

Nick began to giggle. "No. I'm not that hungry either."

They still had a couple of hours before the Greystones were due to leave so they went for a drink in the hotel bar. Dimitri still didn't know anything about what had happened and babbled on about his teacher's house in the city centre.

"There's one thing I do want to know," Mr Greystone said when Dimitri had gone to the toilet. "How did you get Angus out of the cave?"

"I made men scared," Dummie said proudly. "They almost scared to death."

"How then?"

"He showed them his burns and they thought he was a mummy," Angus said.

"A mummy?"

"A living mummy," Angus said.

"Hahaha! Kgrrr! Kgrrr!" Mr Greystone snorted so loudly that everyone in the bar looked up.

"Well, you'd have terrified them just as much with that laugh of yours," Nick grinned.

Then Dimitri came back and they changed the subject.

At four o'clock, Mr Greystone and Dummie got into a taxi van. Nick, Angus and Dummie waved them off. The van turned, drove down the access road and disappeared tooting into the traffic.

"Well. That was that," Nick said in relief. "What are we going to do now?"

"Sleep!" Dummie and Angus cried in unison.

"But first another surprise," said Dummie.

"A surprise? Another one? I've had enough surprises for now," Nick protested.

"No. Must be now," Dummie said.

They took the lift upstairs. In the bedroom, Dummie picked up the bundle of rags he'd been carrying the whole time and got out the camera. "You ghave to see photos of ghrave," he said to Nick.

"Oh, is that the surprise? Oh, but I want to see them," Nick said delightedly. He took the camera and began to look at the pictures. "Whumpy dumpman! Unbelievable. All that gold! Uggh, what scary jars! What a pity I didn't get to see any of this with my own eyes."

Dummie grinned. "You see now," he said.

"Huh?"

"I ghave another surprise. Are you ready?" He laid the bundle of rags down on the bed and unfolded it deferentially.

Angus and Nick grabbed hold of each other. They stared at the long golden object in disbelief. "W-what's that?" Nick stuttered.

"This is from my dad," Dummie said proudly. "Is souvenir. I ghave taken it. This is sceptre of Akhnetut. Do you like?"

Nick opened his mouth and shut it again. "Do I like it? Whumpy dumpman! This isn't a souvenir, it's a

catastrophe! I'm feeling nervous already!"

"What do you mean?" asked Angus.

"A golden sceptre! How are we ever going to get that through customs!" groaned Nick.

The next day they had a long lie-in. In the afternoon, they roamed around Cairo, went to a big market with little stalls that sold everything, and did what all the other tourists do. Dummie didn't want to go to the old city of Memphis anymore, the place he had once lived. He'd found his father's grave and that was enough for him.

On Saturday morning, they rolled up Akhnetut's

sceptre in all the clothes they had and put it in the suitcase amongst the rolls of bandage. They took a taxi and an hour later, they were at Cairo airport.

Nick had already been to the toilet five times, but he had to go again, he said with a desperate look on his face.

"Come on, Dad. We'll be back in Polderdam by this afternoon," Angus said in encouragement.

"If we don't crash," Nick groaned. "Grass, cows, I can't wait. I can tell you this: I don't want anything else to happen for the next ten years."

"Nice and boring," said Dummie.

"Nice and peaceful!" said Nick.

Well, Angus agreed. But with Dummie around, there was never going to be much peace and quiet.

القاهرة

نـجـا هولنديـان من الـموت في الـصـحـراء، بعد أن تاها عن فرقة من السياح راكبين الجمال في صحراء غرب سقـارة، حسب قـولهما. ولقد تم الشروع في البحث عليهما، بعد مكالمة هاتفية قام بها سائح هولندي مجهول. وتم أخيرا العثـور عليهما بفضل قافلة من الرحل. كان الرجلان يعانان من الجفاف و أشعة الشمس. بسبب الهذيان الذي أصابهما، كان بتخيلا ممياءات حية وكهوف خطرة. لقد تم نقلهما إلى مستشفى القاهرة لوضعهما تحت المراقبة. ورغم كل الظروف فقد أصبحا في حالة جيدة. وكالة الأسفار و الفنادق تنصح السياح الأجانب بأن يتوفروا على كثيرا من الماء وخاصة البقاء قريبا من الطرق و أن لا يذهبوا إلى الصحراء وحدهم. ولمذا لم يعملا هذين الرجلين بهذه النصائح و التنبيهات، يبقى عير معروف.

Cairo

**Two Dutch men escaped death in the Sahara. They said
they had become separated from a group of tourists on a
dromedary ride and had got lost in the desert to the west
of Sakkara. A search party was sent out after a worried
telephone call from an anonymous Dutch tourist. They
were eventually found by a caravan of nomads. The men
were dehydrated and suffering from sunstroke. They
ranted and raved about living mummies and dangerous
caves. They were admitted to Cairo hospital for
observation and are doing well given the circumstances.
Travel agencies and hotels always warn tourists to carry
enough water, not to go into the desert on their own
and to stay close to roads at all times. It is not known
why the men ignored this advice.**

ANOTHER BOOK ABOUT DUMMIE THE MUMMY!

Just imagine. You're called Angus Gust, you couldn't be more ordinary and you live in the most boring town in the world. One day, you walk into your bedroom, smell something nasty, look around and suddenly notice a mummy lying in your bed. What would you do? Yes, you would be scared to death, of course. And you would close your eyes, count to ten and be sure it would be gone.

But just imagine that after ten seconds, it would still be there... And after twenty seconds too! What would you do then?